"You're sleeping in the guest room from now on."

"So…no chance even for a quickie right now?" Sawyer teased.

Alana's eyes darkened. "If you keep that up, I'm going to—"

"Tell on me?" Sawyer took another step toward her. Something about her made him edgy and excited. He should just move the rest of his stuff into the guest room and act like a saint.

But he'd never get to touch her again.

Alana glanced to one side, glanced back. Her lips parted.

Where was the outrage now? Swamped by hormones? Was he affecting her the same way she was affecting him?

Worse, her proximity brought back details of the night before. The way she'd arched and moaned, the way her hips had undulated—

"What are you doing?" Her voice came out a cracking whisper. She didn't move away; her eyes held his.

"Trying to keep my promise." *And failing badly.* "Alana, there's nothing to stop you from inviting me to do whatever you want—whenever you want it…."

Dear Reader,

I had so much fun writing this WRONG BED story! It's always a challenge to figure out how to get two strangers into the same bed. But Sawyer and Alana, two irresistible forces, enjoyed themselves so much whether they were arguing or setting the sheets on fire that I felt as if I got to sit back and let them write the book for me. And it's always a pleasure to have my characters inhabiting my home city in Wisconsin.

Don't worry if you get to The End and think I forgot Alana's sister Melanie's happy ending. In May look for *Surprise Me...*, another WRONG BED book featuring a love triangle between Melanie and two very different brothers—the wild and wildly exciting Stoner and the sweet and dependable Edgar.

Which would you choose? Come visit with me at www. IsabelSharpe.com for all my news!

Cheers,

Isabel Sharpe

WHILE SHE WAS SLEEPING…

BY
ISABEL SHARPE

All the characters in this book have no existence outside the imagination of the author, and have no relation whatsoever to anyone bearing the same name or names. They are not even distantly inspired by any individual known or unknown to the author, and all the incidents are pure invention.

First published in Great Britain 2011
Harlequin Mills & Boon Limited,
Eton House, 18-24 Paradise Road, Richmond, Surrey TW9 1SR

© Muna Shehadi Sill 2010

ISBN: 978 0 263 88057 1

14-0211

Harlequin Mills & Boon policy is to use papers that are natural, renewable and recyclable products and made from wood grown in sustainable forests. The logging and manufacturing processes conform to the legal environmental regulations of the country of origin.

Printed and bound in Spain
by Litografia Rosés S.A., Barcelona

Isabel Sharpe was not born pen in hand like so many of her fellow writers. After she quit work to stay home with her first-born son and nearly went out of her mind, she started writing. After more than twenty novels—along with another son—Isabel is more than happy with her choice these days. She loves hearing from readers. Write to her at www.IsabelSharpe.com.

To Stacy, Lisa, Annemarie, Caroline,
Sally, Kris and Joan.
Because it doesn't always have to be
about litera-choor.

1

ALANA HAWTHORNE taped shut her last carton of CDs, mostly jazz and soft rock. The job of packing up her condo hadn't taken long. Everything went into boxes, bang, done. Not like when she'd moved here from her childhood home in suburban Milwaukee and had to decide what to take and what to leave, what belonged to her and what to Melanie, all the while trying not to have unsisterly thoughts, such as could she chain Melanie to a downtown parking meter while she packed?

Moving was easier this time emotionally, too, though she'd lived here outside Chicago for six years. Hard to get sentimental about a condo, even in a building she took pride in managing, a career she'd fallen into after helping her grandfather manage a downtown bank building for so many years. This place had none of the charm of the house in Wauwatosa, none of the leaded glass and gorgeous woodwork. Granted, none of the leaks and drafts and questionable plumbing, either. Or the memories, good and bad, contained in each room of the house she and Melanie were raised in.

This time day after tomorrow, Alana would be in Orlando, Florida, in another condo, in a development she'd be managing. She wasn't wild about the move, considered herself thoroughly Midwestern, but Gran and Grandad had sacrificed a decade of what should have been their much-deserved empty-nest years raising two grandchildren. After Gran's fall last month, it was clear what Alana could do to pay them back at least in some small way.

Her cell rang. She paused to write *CDs—Bedroom* in black marker on the box before scrambling to her feet and grabbing her cell from the oddly bare kitchen counter. The new owners had been impressed by how well she'd kept the place up. Alana didn't mention she'd spent most of her time at Sam's place until they broke up last fall.

She glanced at the display. Her sister. "Hey, Melanie."

"You'll never, ever guess what I have to tell you."

Alana wrinkled her nose. *Hello, Alana, how's the packing going? How's your stress level? Need any help?* "Good news or bad?"

"Good, fabulous, the best, but like I said, you'll never guess."

"You met a guy."

"Oh." Her sister sounded tremendously disappointed. "Well, yes. But not just *a* guy, this is *the* guy."

Alana closed her eyes, dread and fear lifting their little heads inside her, trying to decide if they'd be needed or not. *The* guy, huh? What was this one in recovery from? Or wanted by the police for? Or down on his luck because of? "That's great, Melanie."

"I am *so* excited. He's amazing. What's more, you'll really like this one."

"Where did you meet him?" A meat-market bar at closing time? A bus stop? In court?

"Habitat for Humanity."

Alana turned from her kitchen counter to face the curtain-less window. "No kidding. I didn't know you volunteered for them."

"All part of Melanie's New Improved Life. He's straight,

sober, responsible, an amazing man. Went to college, everything."

"Everything?"

"Everything you think is important."

"Melanie, wow." She actually started feeling hopeful, a huge change from how she usually felt about Melanie's boyfriends, which generally ranked somewhere around despair. "How long have you known him?"

"Long time. A month. Maybe more."

"Really." Hey, Melanie even waited to tell Alana about this one, instead of jumping into I-met-someone-and-love-him after the first date. "This is terrific. I'm happy for you. What's his name?"

"Sawyer Kern."

Even that was normal. Not Spike or Screech, or that one guy who simply went by Dude. "Good name."

"You'll love him." Melanie blew out a breath, which sounded like a storm blast through the phone. "Um, so, I just… Uh, how are things there?"

Alana's eyes narrowed. Um, so, she just…what? "Fine. Nearly packed. Was there something else you were going to say?"

"Oh. Well. It's just a little thing." She laughed nervously. No, it was going to be a big thing. "Ye-e-es?"

"I wanted to tell you. We're…moving in together."

Uh-oh. Yellow alert. "In Gran and Grandad's house?"

"It's our house now, Alana."

"I know, but it…" She gave up. Even though her grandparents sold the house to her and Melanie when they moved to Florida, the place would always be theirs in her heart. "Okay, into *our* house?"

"Yes. I mean, of course you'll have to say it's okay."

"When is he moving in?"

"Um…tomorrow."

Orange alert. Waiting until the last second to tell Alana?

Or did this Sawyer guy wait until the last second to ask Melanie? "You've known him a month? Is that…maybe…rushing things?"

"I know, it seems fast. But it's also really practical."

"Shared bedroom saves gas money?"

Another nervous laugh. "No. He, um, needed a place to live. So I thought this was an obvious solution. To help him out."

"Ah." Homeless guy. Super. Alana let her head bonk back against a cabinet so she was staring up at the smooth, white ceiling. Very uncomfortable position, but it fit the conversation. "Did he get evicted?"

"No, nothing like that. Just…between places, I guess."

She guessed. "He's paying half the expenses, utilities, property tax, etc.?"

"Ye-es, Alana." She sounded like an exasperated teenager. "He promised to share all expenses."

"Did he promise in writing?"

Her sister scoffed. Alana bit her lip. *Don't push too hard.* "What does he do?"

"Oh. Well…"

Red alert. Alana closed her eyes wearily. Male stripper? Female impersonator? Drug dealer?

"He was some kind of lawyer, I guess, but it was too much pressure, so he's between jobs at the moment."

Even better. "How long has he been unemploy—"

"Geez, Alana. I *knew* you'd do this. I'm a *grown-up,* remember? Twenty-six? And you're not my mother."

Oh, no. The last of Alana's hope evaporated. Melanie went on the attack like that when she was feeling defensive. She had something to hide about this guy. Something Alana wouldn't like. "Yes, it's your life. But it's also half my house."

"I *told you,* Alana, he's a great guy, not like the others."

"Really." Alana pulled her head up from the cabinet.

"The last ones were 'not like the others,' too, except for one thing—they were *just* like the others."

"Alana…"

She took a deep breath. She'd moved away from her beloved house and her beloved city partly because of the way she and Melanie got along. Or didn't. That and a job opportunity managing luxury condos for a man who'd known her Grandad. "Okay, I'm sorry. You know I'm just being—"

"Smothering."

"No, cautious. Can you blame me?" She kept her voice gentle. "Seriously? For all I know he's planning to marry you and weasel you out of your half of the house, or take it over for…I don't know, something bad. Invite creepy friends in at all hours who'll trash the place or—"

"He's not like that."

"You said that about the last one. The ex-con who tried to steal the family silver." She shoved herself away from the cabinet, stalked into the living room. Her sister didn't just push her buttons; she hurled grenades and exploded them. In spite of Gran and Grandad's best efforts, Melanie had grown up wild like Alana and Melanie's mother.

Every time Melanie used poor judgment—or, more accurately, *no* judgment—Alana was catapulted back to the fear and bewilderment of her rocky first decade with Mom, before Gran and Grandad took her and her sister in and introduced them to foreign ideas like good nutrition and routine and stability.

"I'm turning over a new leaf. I promise. This guy could run for office."

"Which means he has affairs, hires prostitutes and/or propositions guys in bathrooms?"

"Ha, ha, ha. You know what I mean."

"Yes. I do." *Calm, Alana, calm.* Who knew? Maybe Sawyer was okay. Melanie was a grown-up; her life was her own.

But that beautiful house was half Alana's and, legal issues

aside, she hated the idea of some guy living there who didn't belong, didn't understand how precious a place it was.

Or was Alana being selfish? Unreasonable? She could be both, she knew. If only Melanie didn't have such a dismal record. "Can you just date him a little longer, get to know him better before he moves in?"

"I've known him a month, what more do you want?"

"Two months? Four? Eight? A year?"

"He needs a place now. I've got one."

"*We've* got one." Alana sank down onto the one space on her couch not heaped with boxes and tried to calculate. She could put off traveling to Florida by a day or two. She'd wanted to get to Orlando a couple of weeks early before starting her new job, but she didn't absolutely have to be there yet. Her furniture was going into storage regardless, while she stayed with Gran and Grandad. "Here's an idea. How about if I come up and meet him, and if he's all you say, there will be no problem and I'm fine with him moving in."

"For God's sake, Alana, I'm not twelve."

No, you just act like it sometimes. "I know. But the house is half mine, I think it's understandable I'd want to—"

"I think it's understandable that you should trust your own sister."

"Uh…" Based on what? "What is so bad about me visiting?"

Her red alert got redder. She'd just tossed the idea out there, hadn't really thought it through. Moving was plenty stressful enough, all her plans were in place, she hated to delay. But with Melanie objecting…

"It's just…you shouldn't…we shouldn't have to go through this."

"I'd like to meet him."

"Oh, um, well…"

Alana dropped her head into her hands. This was not good. If Melanie didn't want Alana to meet Sawyer, that was proof positive he was more bad news, and Alana needed to get up to Wauwatosa as soon as possible to protect her childhood home and to prevent her sister from screwing up her life exactly the way she always did. Exactly the way their mother had.

IN THE LAST RAYS of twilight traveling north on I94, the familiar skyline of Milwaukee came into view, unimposing compared to the majestic sprawl of downtown Chicago, but home. Alana got a lump in her throat and wished for her boxed-up camera to take a picture she could frame on her wall in Orlando.

She changed lanes, enjoying the light traffic after her years in bumper-to-bumper Chicago and lowered the window a few inches to breathe warm, summery air. Florida would be sweltering at this time of year. What's more, July was bang in the middle of hurricane season. Two already this year had narrowly avoided the state, another, Cynthia, was forming in the Atlantic.

Alana had called Gran and Grandad to let them know of her change in plans, making it sound like, *Hurray, Melanie found a great guy and Alana couldn't wait to meet him!* She'd added a white lie about needing a few items from the house in case her grandparents got suspicious, knowing Melanie as they did. How many boyfriends had they needed to extract from Melanie's life or steer her around since she hit puberty? They had good practice after raising Alana and Melanie's mom, but still. They shouldn't need to deal with those worries anymore.

Gran had sounded tired, but brushed off questions about her recovery from the fall, saying she was fine. Of course. A building could tip over onto her head and she'd insist no one should be concerned.

Route I94, to Route 41, then west on Lloyd toward Wauwatosa—the city nestled right up to Milwaukee's west side—bumping over the filled potholes pockmarking the street. At

62nd Street, she turned left into The Highlands, a beautiful neighborhood of curving streets graced by elegant old houses. Her grandparents had bought the two-story stone house on Betsy Ross Place in the 1940s when they were first married. Until they moved to Florida six years earlier when Alana graduated from University of Wisconsin-Milwaukee, there they'd stayed.

Right on Washington Circle, left on Betsy Ross, third driveway on the right. Alana pulled in and peered apprehensively up at the house in the near darkness. No lights on. No cars in the driveway. She hadn't told Melanie she'd decided to come. Sneaky, maybe, but the fight on the phone earlier that afternoon would only have gotten uglier.

She stepped from her Prius, inhaling the fresh warm air, and stretched before she got out her suitcase, drinking in the sight of familiar leafy elms and oaks, beautifully manicured lawns, colorfully landscaped yards, stately grand houses lining the shady streets. The garage turned out to be as empty of Melanie's Civic as the driveway, but a beat-up Chevy sat on the street in front of their house—Sawyer's car? Alana grimaced. She hadn't thought about what she'd do if Melanie wasn't home and he was. That could get awkward, especially if she took an instant dislike to him as she did to ninety-eight percent of Melanie's men—the other two percent took a day or two. With luck, Melanie had stopped for a quick drink after work and wasn't on one of her all-night party binges.

Up the front walk to the white-columned portico, her suitcase bumping up the steps, Alana let herself in with the key she hadn't managed to make herself surrender and stood in the hallway, smelling the familiar smells, emotions swirling in her chest. Happiness to be there mixed with funny pangs of knowing she'd be so far away for so long.

On the wall to her left hung the pictures she'd taken on Mom's last sporadic visit, four years earlier on the occasion of Melanie's graduation from UWM, before Mom took off again, presumably for good this time. In her favorite—their picnic on Lake Michigan's Bradford Beach—she'd caught Gran and Grandad, Melanie and Mom in an impromptu group hug, arms around each other, smiling broadly, hair blowing in the wind—except Grandad's because he no longer had any.

Mom—or Tricia, as she wanted her daughters to call her now that they were grown, which they both refused to do—still called on or around their birthdays, still promised to visit "really soon," still sent haphazard thinking-of-you cards and occasional gifts—crystals and bulky, colorful jewelry, books on spiritual healing—that had nothing to do with who they had become.

"Mel?" Alana wandered into the kitchen, glanced around and made a face. Cleaning was not Melanie's forte, though the place wasn't as bad as Alana had found it on her few other visits over the past six years.

She crossed to the refrigerator, a side-by-side beauty that the deliverymen had barely gotten through the kitchen door. Inside…yuck. Classic Mel. A few take-out containers, condiments, a rind of Parmesan cheese, one egg, half a lemon, pale celery, a shriveled apple and about two dozen beers.

Mmm, mmm, good.

An hour later, she'd gone to the supermarket, come back, eaten a slice of very good pre-cooked tenderloin with veggies and fruit from the salad bar, cleaned up after herself and settled into the living room with a book from Grandad's library, which she and Melanie hadn't been able to get rid of.

At eleven, head pounding from tension, Alana closed a book on Charles Lindbergh she wasn't really reading and stood. Odds were good she wouldn't be able to sleep for a while but she didn't want to wait down here anymore. Melanie could easily stay out until two or three. Alana needed her eight hours every night or she turned into a daytime zombie. Sleep to Melanie seemed more like a careless luxury.

Could they be any less alike? Alana's dark to Melanie's light, Alana's lifelong struggle against adding pounds to Melanie's effortlessly slender figure, Alana's practicality and love of order to Melanie's sloppy impulsiveness. They only had her mother's word they had the same father.

So. Alana sighed and started up the curving wooden steps to the second floor, lugging her overnight bag. She'd wanted to get this confrontation—or, optimistically, this *meeting*—over with so she wouldn't have to think about it all night long. Good thing she'd brought sleeping pills, a new, stronger prescription the doctor said should help her relax on nights when she knew drifting off would take chemical help. Tonight was definitely one of those nights.

Upstairs, she pushed open the familiar door to her room and stopped dead. Melanie had removed all her personal items. Her stuffed animals from high school, her gymnastic awards, her ceramic animals bought with childhood allowance from a tiny, now-defunct store on Vliet Street, her floral bedspread and curtains, all gone.

Alana stalked to Melanie's room, which still looked exactly the same as always, except that the bed was actually made. Betty Boop clock and phone, clothes strewn everywhere, makeup cluttering her dresser, jewelry scattered all over her desk among framed photographs and her clumsy teenage attempts at pottery.

Next stop, the master bedroom, which showed clear signs of habitation, including the unmade bed. Melanie and Sawyer must be sleeping here. Next door, the guest room—Mom's girlhood bedroom—was unchanged, twin beds still covered in rose-colored quilts.

What was the deal with Alana's room? Was this Melanie's way of sticking it to her sister? Why not hang a big Alana No Longer Lives Here sign on the front door? At least Mel could have asked if trashing Alana's past was okay.

She slumped against the wall in the hallway, head throbbing, on the verge of tears. Maybe she shouldn't have come.

Except she had to to make sure the house would be taken good care of, and she had to make sure Sawyer wouldn't take Melanie on another one-way ride to heartbreak and/or self-destruction.

She took her makeup kit into the hall bathroom—cleaned recently, thank goodness—brushed her teeth and slugged down a sleeping pill. Tonight at least she'd sleep. Tomorrow she'd deal with all this, when she was refreshed.

But first, something for this headache. She scoured the medicine cabinet and pulled down a bottle of generic ibuprofen, popped the top and shook one into her hand, staring in the mirror while she filled a paper cup from the clouded plastic dispenser with water. She looked tired, dark circles under her eyes and faint puffiness; the stress of the past few days and this damn headache had turned her pale. Ugh.

A split second before she tossed back the pill, she noticed it wasn't ibuprofen's usual brown-orange color. Funny. Most of the generics looked similar to the brand names. She studied the bottle. It *said* ibuprofen... Should she panic?

She was too tired.

Face washed, changed into the cream-colored cotton camisole and girl boxers she wore in the summer, she settled into bed with *A Year of Wonders,* a favorite book from her untouched bookshelf—at least Melanie left that alone.

Within twenty minutes, sleep started to overpower her to the point where her eyes crossed as she struggled vainly to keep them open. Whoa. Those new pills Dr. Bagin gave her were serious.

The book slid off the bed; she couldn't even be bothered to stop its fall. She reached for the light and nearly knocked the lamp off the table.

Sleep. She had to.

Now. No fighting it.

She pulled the covers over her with arms that felt like forty-pound weights.

Very...potent...pills...

2

SAWYER KERN opened his eyes. Had he heard something or dreamed it? He frowned. The ceiling looked wrong. Where was his fan? Who had taken his ceiling fan?

He lifted his head, grimacing at the effort. What the—

The room wasn't remotely familiar. Where the hell was he? How did he *get* here? He couldn't remember a damn thing.

His head dropped back; he tried to focus his fuzzy brain, which didn't want to focus at all. Was he still dreaming? He didn't think so.

Party…okay, yes, he'd been at a party. His brother Finn threw a coed bachelor party for a friend at a local bar. Right. That was it. He'd had a few drinks. More than usual. Some kind of vodka he thought, mixed with other stuff. His head still didn't feel right. Too big. Or maybe too small.

Wait. He hadn't had *that* many, had he? He'd never been blacked-out drunk in his life. Never. Not even close. Spins a few times, that was it.

But somehow he'd ended up here. Wherever here was. He squinted, frowning, trying to concentrate.

Wait. Something else was coming to him. At the party. Last thing he remembered he'd been talking to a beautiful brunette. A very hot beautiful brunette. An artist. No, she was in insurance. No. Both? Neither? He remembered thinking she was being *aw*-fully friendly and he remembered not minding at all. It had been a while since a woman came on to him.

Then…yes, someone had offered him another drink, a different one, "specialty of the house." Whatsisname, Finn's friend from college, from the group which never managed to graduate mentally from fraternity days. The one Sawyer never liked or trusted.

Still, he'd accepted. One more drink wouldn't hurt, that's what he'd thought, but then he'd stop. How many total? Three? Four? Not more.

The brunette had declined, rolling her eyes. Sawyer had decided from something the fraternity jerk said that he and the brunette had a past, that her interest had ended but his hadn't. What was her name? Deb? Debbie? Deborah? Something.

He'd had the drink, was chatting with Deb…whatever. And then…

Nothing. Nothing after that.

What the hell had he…*Phil,* that was his name. Phil. What had been in that drink? More than alcohol. Something that completely—

He heard the sound again. The one that woke him. A low sigh/moan, the kind a woman makes when she's aroused.

Uh-oh. He turned his head and saw the outline of a shoulder against the barest glow from a streetlight creeping in around the shades. Speaking of the hot brunette. He must have gone home with her.

No. He looked around the room again; this time the details clicked. He'd brought her to Melanie's. He remembered that much now. He'd known better than to drive, so he'd walked here. Melanie had already given him a key to the house.

Okay, regroup.

So…this incredible artist-or-insurance-agent brunette had agreed to come home with him even wasted to the point where he could barely function?

Wow. On a very shallow "guy" level, he was quite impressed with himself. She hadn't had the "specialty of the house" spiked with God knew what, so her decision must have been based on actual rational thought. Or as rational as thought could get when hormones took control.

So, hey. He'd left thirty behind a couple of years ago, but he wasn't dead yet.

His one-night stand stirred and rolled to her back, head turned away from him. Funny, he remembered her hair shorter. But then who knew what had happened to his mind last night?

And while he was at it, who knew what had happened to his body? Whatever it was—and from the hungry way she'd looked at him it promised to be good—he couldn't believe he'd missed it.

He turned on his side, gazing down at what he could see of her. She smelled good. Womanly and fresh. He hadn't noticed last night in the crowded room. Maybe she wouldn't mind a replay of whatever they did when they got here. He was still under the influence of something, but this time he was pretty sure he'd remember the whole thing.

"Hey. Deb...bie...orah."

"Mmph." She moved again, turned toward him. The sheet slid off her shoulder to reveal the top few inches of a low-cut and very sexy clingy camisole which she filled out much better than he'd have thought from the slender frame he remembered. He hadn't even undressed her? Had they been in that much of a frantic hurry? Damn, why couldn't he remember?

Unless...nothing had happened. Maybe he'd completely humiliated himself by not being able to perform under the influence of whatever jerk-Phil spiked that last drink with. He hoped he'd at least made something happen for her.

Maybe he hadn't even been able to do that. Maybe that was Phil's plan.

He cringed. This time he'd do everything right. His body was already reacting, just to her nearness.

"Deb." He traced her plunging neckline with a gentle finger.

"Mmm." She frowned and pursed her lips, which were gray in the dim light, but which he remembered as red and full, the kind you wanted to kiss the second you saw them.

"You're beautiful," he whispered. "Even more beautiful than last night when I could see you."

That didn't come out right. His brain was definitely still muddled. But another part of his body was wide-awake and full of a very clear purpose. She looked like a black-and-white movie star, her skin the creamy end of gray where it had been gold in the light, her hair jet-black where it had been reddish brown. Cream-gray breasts, black shadow between them. His lips found the spot; her soft, round flesh embraced his jaw.

She gave a soft moan that made him want to grab her camisole and tear it off with his teeth. Instead, he moved his hand up her strong, firm calf, over the swell of her hamstring to the firm rounding of her ass, which had filled out jeans in a way that could bring grown men to tears.

He still couldn't believe this incredible woman had come home with him. Er, to his temporary home. With Melanie.

Uh-oh. He hadn't cleared the bringing-women-home thing with her. He hoped she wouldn't be upset. Not like it would happen all the time.

Debbie moaned again as his fingers explored underneath her soft low-slung boxers, and he decided to worry about the details later. Melanie was a big girl. She'd handle it. Right now he had a woman to wake up and enjoy.

He slid her straps down and his tongue found her nipple, which he investigated thoroughly, then moved to the other. His fingers found moisture between her legs, probed and teased up and down the crevice, still reaching from behind her.

Her head lifted briefly from the pillow; her lips parted. Her eyes stayed closed.

She had to be pretending. No one could sleep through being touched like this. And he could tell by her occasional gasps and irregular breathing that he wasn't exactly boring her to sleep.

Unless she'd had some "specialty of the house" at some point later in the evening and was still blacked out while responding subconsciously to him?

Kinky. He loved it.

Though if she hadn't come home with him in her right mind, it would be pretty ungentlemanly of him to take advantage of her senseless state now by making love to her.

Wouldn't it.

Could he open the window and throw his conscience out?

Except…if he pleasured *her,* there was no taking advantage. He was dying to taste her, to keep touching her and torturing himself with her desire. She'd been so sexy to him just standing there at the party. Writhing and turned on in his bed? Ten times more.

Sawyer tugged aside the material of her very feminine boxers until she was bared to him. He burrowed under the covers, drew his mouth down her stomach, farther down, then lowered his lips to taste her.

Warm. Soft. Sweet. He took his time, moving slowly, circling here, thrusting there, enhancing his tongue's rhythm with his fingers inside her, feeling the warm smooth walls grabbing, his cock begging to be in on the trip.

She responded with tiny whimpers that undid him, lifting her hips dreamily, lowering them in surrender, her motions sleepy and graceful.

He stopped his exploration, settled into a regular rhythm, gradually accelerating the pace and pressure, thrusting his fingers, swirling his tongue until he felt her tense, felt her orgasm grow and come on slowly almost as if he were experiencing it himself. She gave a muffled cry, her hips bucked once, held tight, suspended, then those smooth walls contracted tightly around his fingers.

Oh, man. He let her down slowly, his breathing harsh, so turned on it was all he could do not to plunge into her and let himself go. Her eyes were still closed; she frowned slightly, as if in confusion, arched so a breast spilled from the thin cotton.

Last straw. He pulled his fingers gently from her, knelt on the bed and grabbed his cock, manipulating it swiftly, watching her, focusing on her body, on her full breasts, on the way her nipples were still upright, pulling the areola close around them, then down to her waist, lower to where her dark curls lay, so recently against his chin...

On the edge and starting to feel like a pervert voyeur, he closed his eyes, imagining her sex still underneath his mouth.

He stifled a groan, held his other hand at the ready, and came into it in strong hot bursts, the image of her body burned into his memory so deeply this time he was sure if he lived to be one hundred, it would never be erased.

Wow. He pursed his lips, exhaled. Wow.

"Debbie."

No response. He smiled, got off the bed and headed for the bathroom. This had been an unusual, er, episode, unexpected and slightly twisted. But for some reason he was hurrying through his cleanup, anxious to get back to her. Was that the ultimate guy thing? Feeling warm and affectionate toward a woman who couldn't talk back? Who wasn't even conscious? Didn't they make some movie about a guy in love with a sex doll?

Nice. He chuckled, washed his hands, drank a paper cup of water, found a bottle of generic ibuprofen for a headache that wasn't all that bad, then noticed tiny printing in permanent marker—Joe's pills.

Never mind.

In the room, he covered Debbie carefully and crawled in beside her, hoping when she woke up she remembered who he was and why she was here. Because he was about ninety-nine percent sure that in the morning he'd want to do it all again and more, this time with her full erotic participation.

ALANA SMILED, awake, but only barely, and not nearly ready to open her eyes yet. Mmm. She'd slept like a log, and what a *won*-derful dream. An incredibly sexy stranger had gone down on her right here in her bed. She could remember so clearly the warm feel of his tongue and the insistent push of his fingers inside her. The guy knew exactly what he was doing. She'd love to meet someone like that in real life, no offense to Sam, her old boyfriend, who wasn't big on, um, oral traditions.

The imagined feeling had been so amazing and so vivid she'd actually climaxed. Usually when she was aroused in a dream she'd get ri-i-ight to the brink, then wake up before the final rush, frustrated and horny. But last night, mmm, no problem all the way from A to Z. If that's what those new sleeping pills did, she'd take them every night.

She managed to get her eyes open a slit, enough to see sunshine pouring in around the shades in her old room. She used to lie here as a child and imagine herself—

Her body went rigid.

Oh my God.

Someone just moved behind her.

Hardly daring to breathe, she turned over...

Gah! She flung herself over the edge of the mattress, turned and stared, panting, hand to her chest. There was a man in her bed. God, last night...what...how could she...who...

She dragged the spread from the bed and wrapped it around

herself. The blood rushed from her head; she bent over before she passed out, keeping her forehead low.

What. The. Heck.

Was that not a dream?

She was going to be sick.

Had a complete stranger actually *taken advantage* of her while she was *asleep?*

She coughed a few times to get the blood solidly back in her brain, then raised her head slowly and carefully, forcing her breath down deep so she wouldn't hyperventilate.

Bastard. Whoever he was…

"Hey." She gave the mattress a good kick to jiggle Prince Not-At-All Charming awake. *"Hey."*

His eyes opened. She kicked the mattress again. He turned and squinted in annoyance. "Why are you kicking my bed?"

"This is *my* bed."

"Uh." He looked around in confusion. "I don't…"

"Who are you?"

He stared as if she'd lost her mind, then shook his head. "Oh, no. You did have that drink."

"Whah?"

"The one you told me not to have, Phil's 'specialty of the house.' It does something to your brain."

She stared blankly. Oh my God. A complete psycho. Clearly one of Melanie's friends. "I was not drinking last night."

"The bachelor party for Dan? Thrown by my brother, Finn Kern?"

"I don't know anyone named—"

"We talked for a long while." His eyes narrowed. He had the gall to look her up and down. "Though, actually, you do look different than I remember."

"I have *no idea* who you are."

"Sawyer Kern? Ring any bells?"

"Sawyer!?" She gasped, practically inflating with outrage

on her sister's behalf. This...this predator was Melanie's The One? The guy who was different from all the rest?

"I guess you do remember."

"You...you're Melanie's..."

His eyes narrowed. "You know Melanie?"

"I'm her *sister*." *Oh, Melanie.* Alana had been stupid enough to hope this guy *would* be different.

"Alana?" He hoisted himself to sitting, rubbed his face as if trying desperately to make himself wake up the rest of the way. She refused to notice that his chest was broad and magnificent. Or that his lips were full and masculine and had been between her...never mind. "What were you doing at the bachelor party?"

"I wasn't at the party."

He appeared to process that for a while.

"So I didn't pick you up there, bring you here and then forget." He chuckled, shaking his head. "I knew I couldn't have been that out of it."

How could he find anything about this situation funny? "You came home and crawled into *bed* with *me*. In *this room*."

"I drank something pretty strong and didn't notice you." He turned his deep brown eyes on her face. "That is, I didn't notice you at *first*..."

His smile became suggestive and secretive. Alana took a step back, clutching the bedspread, feeling a massive blush coming on even while thinking, *Oh, great, not just a womanizer, a blacking-out* alcoholic *womanizer.* Her sister never did anything by halves. "I took a sleeping pill and didn't wake up until this morning. Just now. Not before. Slept all night. All of it."

He grinned at her confusion. "You don't remember... anything?"

"Of course not. I was asleep."

"Hmm, I better fill you in, then, because I remember a

whole lot of what happened around 3:00 a.m. You were lying there, and I—"

"No. Don't." She waved furiously, stop stop *stop,* then had to grab the bedspread covering her before it fell.

"Huh?" His face was pure innocence. "You don't want to know? I should think that would be pretty important."

"I…" Enter massive blush. "I know that you were…I mean, you were definitely…there, but…"

"But?"

"I, er, thought I was dreaming."

One eyebrow went up over a mischievous eye. "Sweet dream?"

"Not in the slightest." Her voice shook; her blush deepened.

"Hmm, that's not how I remember it. You practically lifted off the—"

"We are not going to discuss this."

"No?" He raised his hand like a schoolboy with a question, rumpled and sexy in her childhood bed. "I need to say something."

Argh. "Go ahead."

"I was drunk, you were drugged, we both have excuses. Let's just start over." He patted the sheets next to him. "Come back to bed."

"What?" She could not believe she'd actually heard him say that. *"You know I'm Melanie's sister and you want me back in bed?"*

"Geez." He clutched his head and glared. "Melanie told me you were strung like a piano wire. Could you not shriek quite so loud—"

"I'll shriek as damn loudly as I want to. I knew you'd be like this. Like all the others. That's why I came."

"That's" why you came? I thought my technique had something to do with that."

She was not amused. At all. His wink did nothing to her.

At all. Even though it was atrociously sexy. "I *arrived here* to protect her. And you, you jump into bed with me and do God knows what. And by the way, piano wires are strung tight so they can play at their best."

"If you say so."

"Now please get out of my room so I can—"

"Your room? Melanie set this room up for me. She had no idea you were coming, or if she did, she didn't tell me."

"Oh, well, no. She didn't know." Alana frowned. Something about this made no sense. "But…why aren't you in the master bedroom with her?"

His eyebrows raised again. "Why would—"

"Alana!?" Melanie's blond head poked around the door, expression incredulous. "What the hell are you—"

She saw Sawyer in the bed and gasped. "Oh my *God*."

"No." Alana put both hands out toward her sister.

"You *slept* with Sawyer last night?" she shrieked.

Sawyer helped the situation not at all by clutching his head in his hands and groaning, which made him look guilty and contrite instead of hungover and tired of shrieking.

"Melanie, this is not at all what it looks—"

"Give me a break." She came out from around the door, wearing a wrinkled short skirt and top she'd obviously slept in, and took two menacing steps forward, hands jammed on her hips, hazel eyes flashing. "Okay, I'll tell you what it looks like, Alana, and you let me know how on target I am. You slept with Sawyer last night."

"No, I didn't. I swear." She realized that she was standing there with bed-head, wrapped in a bedspread, mostly bare shoulders showing, and that Sawyer was still half under the covers, clearly just awake and naked from the waist up, so her words wouldn't carry much weight. "Sleeping, okay, sleeping, but that's it, and that wasn't on purpose. He got into bed with me. I didn't even wake up."

"You know, that's the nicest thing a woman has ever said to me."

She glared at him. He was smirking, the jerk. He'd cheated on Melanie with a member of her own family and thought this whole thing was amusing? "You're not helping."

He put his hand up to block his mouth from Melanie's view. "You want me to tell her what you can do in your sleep?"

"Shh." She looked around. Any weapons? Blunt or otherwise?

"What are you whispering about?" Melanie shrieked. Shrieking must run in their family. Alana had never noticed before.

"State secrets." He turned to Melanie. "Alana is correct. She slept all night. I thought she was someone else when I woke up."

"You mix up women in bed?" Alana snorted. "Impressive."

Melanie looked crestfallen. "I didn't realize you were that type when I asked you to move in, Sawyer."

"No, I meant…" He sighed. "I'm just saying. If I knew she was your sister, I never would have—"

"Stayed." Alana nodded at her sister. If he said *anything* about what he did to her, she'd show him what shrieking could sound like. She'd have a talk with Melanie later and bring it up only if Melanie needed proof the guy was a sleazeball. Why hurt her more? "If he knew I was me, he would have run. Far."

"That's for sure." He rolled his eyes. "Very far."

Alana ignored him. She was damn glad she'd delayed her trip to Florida and showed up here, because her sister definitely needed saving from Sawyer. If Melanie thought this guy was even close to someone she should get serious about…

Melanie's face crumpled; she hid her face in her hands. "I can't believe you did this."

Alana and Sawyer exchanged glances. Sawyer pointed to

himself, then to Alana, then shrugged, hands up. Which one did she mean?

Alana pointed emphatically at him. *Give her a break.*

"Why did you come here?" Melanie raised her tear-stained face, mascara already smudged from sleep making black tracks down her cheeks. "I told you not to."

Alana gaped. *She* was in trouble? Oh, that was just special. "I came so I could—"

"And now look what *you've* done." Melanie gestured to Sawyer.

"What *I've* done?" He poked himself in the chest. "You're mad at *me?*"

"You slept with my sister."

He put his hands to his ears. "I did not realize she was your sister."

"Ha!" Alana turned on him. "Like that makes any difference?"

"I'm sorry, did I take some vow of chastity I'm not aware of?" He had the gall to look bewildered. A sociopath, devoid of a conscience. Add that one to the other two and you got Womanizing Alcoholic Sociopath. The triple crown. Except don't forget *unemployed,* which made it a home run, round all four base flaws.

Alana strode across the room, nearly tripping on the bedspread, took Melanie's shoulder and steered her to the door. "C'mon, Mel. Let's get out of here. Give Mr. Kern lots of privacy to dress and hardly any time to get the hell out of here."

She led her sister down the hall, more angry and shaken up than she'd been in a long time. She hated that she'd been so vulnerable and had responded so thoroughly to Sawyer instead of punching him in the jaw and throwing him out of the house.

The worst part? Standing there just now, wanting to throttle him for the way he'd taken advantage of both her and Melanie, a stupid hormonal part of her had been taking in his muscled body, warm and alive against the white sheets, his vivid brown eyes and strong, handsome features. No matter how much her brain said *jerk, jerk, jerk* this other part had only managed to come up with *mmm-more*.

She needed to buy a marital aid. The largest they had. A plug-in that would dim the lights for blocks and give her an orgasm the size of Cleveland. Then her ridiculous libido should be happy and stop bugging her about a man who wasn't worth her toenail clippings.

In a way she was glad this fiasco had happened, because it made her job so much easier. Sawyer had shown his true colors. *Hello, I'm a horse's butt.* End of story. He was history. Even Melanie had to see that.

Now Alana could go back to her original plan, head out later on today with a clear conscience, having done her big-sisterly duty here. In two days she'd be in Orlando and could start her granddaughterly duty there.

3

MELANIE WAS GETTING READY to blow. She could not believe, not be-*lieve* that her darling big sister, Alana, had once again showed up to take over her life and tell her how she was screwing up. Most people only had one mother. Melanie had three: her real mother, who was sort of around for her first eight years, her grandmother, who raised her after that, and her big sister, who was a giant, bossy pain in her rear. Such a lucky girl.

This time she had to make it clear to Alana that she was twenty-six, not twelve. That she had really sworn off losers and had really found a decent man, and if Alana screwed it up…

She whirled on her sister. "You just had to come up here. You couldn't trust that I—"

Alana put a finger to her lips and pushed open the door to Melanie's childhood room, which Melanie saw through Alana's eyes and realized looked like the room of a…twelve-year-old. Dammit. She'd been keeping it neat, forcing herself to pick up every night before bed, but last night after drinks with coworkers Jenny and Edgar, she'd needed an outfit for Ray's get-together and hadn't been able to decide what to wear, tried on everything she owned, then it got late, and—

No. She wasn't going to be defensive anymore. She lived her life honestly and it was her own damn business how she kept her room.

"Melanie." Alana shut the door behind her, glanced around, but miracle of miracles, didn't make her usual face and comment about pigs. Okay, she'd only done that once, when Melanie was thirteen. But it still hurt.

"Alana." She held her head high, wishing she were wearing jeans and a sweater instead of her revealing rumpled outfit from the night before. She'd been so tired when she got home around four, she'd dropped right into bed, and slept until Alana's and Sawyer's voices woke her. "You have twenty seconds to explain why when I told you I found a great guy, you drove straight up here and seduced him."

"That is *not* what happened." She dropped the bedspread, grabbed a loose skirt and teal sweater from Melanie's floor.

"You did drive straight up here."

"Yes. I did." She pulled on the skirt, which barely fit over the curvy hips Melanie wished she had, dragged the too-tight sweater over her generous boobs, ditto. "I was worried about you."

"So the phrases 'I've changed' and 'this guy is different'... you thought I was lying? Or so stupid that I had no idea what I was talking about?"

"What is so great about a guy who makes a move on your sister?"

"I thought you said all that went on was sleeping."

Alana's face went blank. She slumped against the wall and knocked off Melanie's firefighters calendar. Mr. July was muscled enough to go bodysurfing on, but he fell without protest. "I wasn't going to tell you."

"Why?"

"Because what was the point of hurting you more?"

She looked so miserable Melanie had to force herself to

calm down. She knew Sawyer wasn't a player, but then Alana wasn't, either. So… "What *did* happen?"

"I was asleep. My doctor gave me new pills and then Sawyer…I thought I was dreaming."

"Come on. You slept through sex?"

"We didn't have sex. He just—"

"Ew." Melanie put her hands out. "I don't want to know."

"But also, I had a headache and took one of the ibuprofen in the medicine cabinet. It didn't look right, and I wondered if maybe I was *so* asleep because—"

"Oh, gosh." Melanie's eyes widened. "I wondered where those were. That wasn't ibuprofen, those were sleeping pills I borrowed from Joe."

"Whoa." Alana's eyebrows shot up. "I guess *that's* how you sleep through sex."

"I thought you said—"

"No." She waggled her finger back and forth. "I meant it. No sex. But the guy is bad news, Melanie."

Here we go. Mommy Alana on a roll. "He didn't know who you were."

"What was he doing making a pass at *anyone* if you're dating seriously?"

"Oh." Melanie did everything she could not to look guilty. They weren't exactly dating yet. But he'd shown interest moving in with her, hadn't he? And with the two of them together so much, something would happen. He was perfect for the new her. But if she told Alana she'd asked Sawyer to move into their house when she'd only seen him four times briefly at Habitat for Humanity, Alana would stay for the rest of Melanie's life. "Well…he was drunk. He didn't know what he was doing."

"And this is an excuse why? For one thing, blacking-out drunk is serious. For another, alcohol doesn't force you to cheat."

"Look. Just drop it, okay? Sawyer and I have worked this

out. He's moving in today and that's what we both want. I've never seen him drink too much before, this was probably a one-time overindulgence. And if not, I'll keep an eye out and handle it, okay?"

"No, not okay. I don't want you getting involved with someone—"

"Who you don't know at all and who has a perfectly reasonable explanation for how he behaved? It's actually more reasonable than yours." She wanted to turn into a bear, growl and terrify Alana out of the house, then shred a tree or something. She couldn't stand the fighting. It was all they did. "Tell you what. I'll put him on probation for a month."

"Melanie, I can't believe—"

"One month." She held up a finger. "Any signs of excessive drinking or, um, cheating on me again, and I'll throw him out. In the meantime, while you're here, you make an effort to talk to him and get to know him when he hasn't been drinking, which I'm telling you is *not* like him. If you still think he's a jerk, then we'll talk. But I know you won't."

Alana sighed, pushed herself away from the wall and re-hung Mr. July, which shouldn't have been necessary since he was plenty well hung already. "Okay. I know I'm a buttinsky. I just worry about you."

"Ya *think?*" She couldn't help grinning. Her sister did look worried, and Melanie was aware a lot of the worry was love. She just wished Alana would keep her worry and love safely long distance. "I'm fine, really. You and Sawyer got off on... okay, rephrase, *started* off on the wrong foot, but he's really terrific. Practically a Boy Scout. I don't know where he was last night, but—"

"You don't?" Alana pounced. "He doesn't tell you where he's—"

"Alana..."

"Okay." She lifted her hands. "Okay, okay. Shutting up. Where were you last night?"

"I went out for a drink after work with Jenny and Edgar. Came back to change, then Jenny and I went to a party."

"Ah." Alana looked at her watch, doubtless thinking, *You're too old to be partying this hard at your age, young lady.* "You don't have work today?"

Melanie whirled around, peered at her Betty Boop clock and gasped. "Oh, God. I'm late."

She started peeling off her clothes, looking desperately around at her discarded wardrobe. What to wear, what to wear.

"I'll find you something for breakfast." Alana left the room before Melanie could tell her she didn't eat breakfast. Whatever. Mommy Alana wouldn't listen anyway. She'd lecture on the importance of a good nutritious start to the day and whip up oatmeal with prunes. Melanie hated oatmeal. And she hated prunes.

Fifteen minutes later, dressed in beige pants and an olive-patterned top she'd bought on sale and never worn because it made her look sallow, teeth brushed, makeup on, stairs leaped down two at a time, she managed not to roll her eyes at the spread on the table. Toast, cereal, power bars, peanut butter, cheese…

"You eat like this every morning?" She grabbed a power bar to keep the peace.

"That color looks horrible on you."

"Thank you." She relented when her sister looked contrite. "I know, but it's the only thing I found that didn't need ironing, and *don't say* that if I kept my clothes hanging in the closet they wouldn't get wrinkled."

Alana looked startled, then drew her fingers across her lips, *zzzip.* "Have a good day at work, dear."

Melanie giggled. "Thank you. Have fun with Sawyer. Try to stay out of bed with him, okay?"

Alana scowled. "He's gone already. Never to return, if he knows what's good for him."

He'd be back. But Melanie wasn't going to say that or risk starting another fight. She rushed to the door, rushed back and grabbed her purse. "I'll be home for dinner. We can go to Gilles for burgers and custard. I know you didn't get enough fat down there in Chicago-town. Bye!"

She didn't wait for her sister to tell her the exact calorie and cholesterol count of her planned dinner. Outside she hauled out her cell, dialed Edgar at Triangle Graphics where she worked downtown in the Third Ward. "Edgar, I'm late."

"That was noticed."

"I know, I know, fifth time this week and it's Friday. I'm on my way, can you charm everyone for me?"

"What's wrong?"

Melanie blinked. He was psychic. He had to be. She couldn't imagine she'd shown any of her confusion and upset, but he always knew. "Nothing! All is good. Be there soon, bye!"

She shut her phone, climbed into her ten-year-old blue Civic and started it up. Good old dependable Honey the Honda. Fifteen minutes later, only breaking a few speed limits, she pulled into the company parking lot, slammed Honey's door and ran inside the renovated warehouse, bumping into—of course—the president of Triangle Graphics, Mr. We-Must-Be-Punctual, Todd Maniscotto.

"Hey, Todd, sorry I'm late. Sister visited unexpectedly, fouled up my whole morning…" *By sleeping with the guy I plan to marry.*

"Good morning." Todd gave her a look over his bifocals and went back to studying whatever design brownnose Bob Stevens was hoping to be praised for.

Melanie scooted into the back room and into her cubicle, grinning hello to Edgar who sat next to her. He looked particularly horrible in a mustard-yellow shirt with brown pants. She'd love to hire herself out as his personal shopper. Obviously his girlfriend didn't know or didn't care about fashion *faux pas* for guys with his dark hair and pale face.

"Hi, Mel. The staff meeting was postponed until ten-thirty today. You got lucky."

She went limp with relief, then stared at the Starbucks cup on her desk. "What's this?"

"Thought you'd need it."

"Edgar." She picked up the cup, sipped experimentally. Mmm, mocha frappucino with extra whipped cream, her very favorite. "You are the absolute sweetest."

"Yeah, I know." He smiled at her. He had a nose the size of a potato, bushy eyebrows, a weak chin, helmet-hair that looked coarse and greasy even when he'd just washed it, the bluest most surprisingly beautiful eyes and a dazzling white-toothed smile. Like matinee-idol mistakes in a nerd movie-designed face. "So tell me what's going on, Melly. You sounded like a wreck on the phone."

"Oh, Ed." She collapsed into her chair, scooted it toward him and told the whole bizarre adventure of the previous evening. "So now my sister spent last night with my intended true love."

"You really like this guy, huh." He stopped moving the mouse, tapped his finger on it without clicking. "More than the others."

"Oh. Well, yes. I mean, I hope to. What's not to like?"

"Uh." He folded his arms across his chest. "That doesn't answer my question."

"Edgar, I'm trying. I'm really trying here. I can't screw up again. I can't keep falling for these toxic guys and then needing to be rescued, either by you or Gran and Grandad or even, bless her to hell, my overlord and sister, Alana. This guy is fabulous. He's handsome, upstanding, no illegal or self-destructive habits, he's sweet as hell…" She sighed.

"And he does nothing for you."

"I'm going to fall for him. He's moving in, something is bound to happen, you know me."

"Um…" He broke out his killer smile. "No comment."

"And after it does, well, I always fall for guys I sleep with. And then I'll be fine. And safe. And set." She eyed her coffee sadly. "Or that's the plan anyway. Pretty stupid, huh."

"It's…better than some of them."

"Eddie," she ducked her head, whispering. "You want to know something?"

"Of course I do."

"I'm scared."

"What do you mean?" He pushed back his chair, put his hand over hers, searched her face. "What is it?"

"What am I going to do if I don't fall for him?" She gazed at him mournfully. "What if I'm doomed to love only danger-ous, emotionally unavailable messes? What if I'm like my mother?"

"You're not like your mother."

"How do you know? You've never met my mother."

"I've heard about her. You're never going to hurt people you love the way she did."

"Thank you, Edgar." She sighed. He was amazing, like he had a guidebook: *Best Things to Say to Melanie.* "Am I ever this nice to you?"

"Always. Emma is jealous of how much I talk about you."

She laughed. "Emma is a lucky woman. Tell her I said so."

"I don't know, she might scratch my eyes out."

"Very doubtful." She squeezed his hand and rolled back to her cubicle. "Was she home when you got back after we had drinks?"

"Yeah, she was there."

"She wasn't angry you'd been out after work?"

"A little, but only because she missed me." He clicked the mouse a few times to change the size of a graphic on his screen. "We hung out on the couch and watched TV to-gether."

Melanie sighed wistfully. That was the kind of evening she should be having instead of partying her brains out. But being still and quiet was an open invitation to demons of self-doubt to start torturing her, so she kept moving. Maybe with Sawyer… "Oh, but when it's the right person, anything is exciting."

"True." He laughed as if he'd thought of something funny.

"What?"

"Nothing. Stop worrying. If your instincts are right about this Sawyer guy…"

"I hope they are. Or will be. I'm just not feeling it, you know? One look at a man who's bad for me and I light up like a winning slot machine. This man is perfect and all I feel for him is determination. I mean, he was in bed last night with my sister and all I felt was annoyed that she'd barged in on my life again. Shouldn't I have been raging jealous?"

"Hell, yeah."

She studied him, intrigued by his vehemence. "So if you came home and found Emma all over another man you'd go nuts?"

"The fur would be flying."

Melanie blew her bangs out of her eyes; they flew up and came right back down again. "That's what I thought."

"Look, you are a beautiful, smart, incredible woman, and there's no way you'll let yourself be dragged into anything permanent with a real creep. This is just a…phase or something."

"I hope so." She put her purse in her file cabinet drawer, took another sip of the rich, sweet coffee and powered on her computer. "I can just see me sixty years from now chasing motorcycle gangs in my wheelchair."

"Well…" He grinned lopsidedly. "You could, you know… try a wider range of nice guys. In case this one doesn't work. Sawyer's not the only nonloser around."

"True." She smiled at him. As usual he'd found a way to make her feel better. "You're absolutely right, Edgar, thank you so much. I'm being ridiculously pessimistic. This is my first attempt at a new life, and I can't expect to hit it right, boom, immediately. Though, I'll tell you, I have not, by any means, no way, given up on Sawyer. I still bet we can get something good going."

She scooted to the right again, leaned forward and kissed Edgar's cheek, making him blush fiercely, which she got a kick out of. He was such a great friend, always seemed to know when she was upset, really listened when she talked to him, anticipated her needs, sometimes before she knew she needed anything. Like the coffee this morning. If he wasn't already involved with Emma, Melanie would try to set him up with one of her friends. Jenny maybe, who was dating that weird sculptor who was horrible to her. Melanie would think she should match *herself* up with Edgar if she felt anything but friendly toward him. Sad to say, once again, when faced with a great guy, Melanie had absolutely no interest.

If she couldn't get herself to fall at least a little bit in love with an incredible man like Sawyer, she was very much afraid she was doomed.

4

SAWYER OPENED his eyes warily…and breathed a sigh of relief. His ceiling fan rotated silently above his bed. This was good. He was home, exactly where he was supposed to be. Even better, he remembered getting here, high-tailing it away from Betsy Ross Place when sweet Melanie and her complete-opposite sister shut themselves away to male-bash, and driving across town to Whitefish Bay on Milwaukee's northeast side, where he fell into bed. Now, his mind was sharp, he felt decently well rested, and he was alone in bed, though he definitely wouldn't have minded waking up next to the Sleeping Beauty version of Alana again.

Having seen her in action awake, however, he had a feeling his stay at Melanie's would go more smoothly if big sister relocated to Florida sooner rather than later. Judging by Melanie's shocked reaction, Alana's visit was a surprise detour. Maybe he'd delay moving in until she was gone.

He'd think about it.

A big yawn, a stretch, and Sawyer let his body relax again, blissfully. He sure as hell did not miss having to get up at 6:00 a.m., rush to work out, shower, shave, put on a suit and fight traffic to be downtown at the office by eight. Nor did he miss the long hours, the pressure, the office politics or the bad coffee. At the same time, the driving sense of purpose had been invigorating. In his world now, it was summertime and the living was always easy. An adjustment, more than he'd expected. Sometimes it felt too easy. Certainly his three brothers and his father were disgusted with his choice to quit his job and take some slow-down time to reevaluate his life. The Kern family never slowed down. Much more honorable to drive oneself into an early grave than give up chasing the almighty dollar. The irony was that the family, descended from the world's third-largest brewing company, Dalton Brewing, had plenty of money already.

Until this year, he'd bought into the family ethic in actions if not in his heart, given up his passion for cabinetry and gone to law school, gotten a Good Job in the Right Firm, same as his engineer, investment banker and doctor brothers, ignoring how he loathed every minute. Heart-attack symptoms last winter landed him in the hospital with a diagnosis of acute stress. Instead of jumping back on the horse, Sawyer promised himself he'd take six months off guilt-free to repair his exhausted body and brain before he committed to the next phase of his life, whatever that would entail. *Not* going back to practicing law.

He sighed. In the meantime, being the black sheep of the family had kept him busy enough, volunteering for Habitat for Humanity and indulging in woodworking again—both on his own in his basement shop and teaching classes through the rec department—visiting museums, reading, making time for concerts, nights out with friends, travel...indulging all the interests he hadn't had time for when his whole world consisted of an office during the day and this bed at night.

He rolled to sitting, glad when his stomach stayed steady and his head stayed clear, though it still throbbed. His cell rang on the clunky bedside table he made in junior high school, which he was replacing with one he'd half finished.

His brother. "Hey, Finn."

"Good, you survived the night."

"Apparently." He cut off a yawn. "What the hell did I drink, and is Phil in jail yet?"

"Police are involved. Yeah, Phil is strongly suspected."

"Nice."

"Listen, Dad called me this morning."

Sawyer rolled his eyes. Mom and Dad had moved to Arizona last year, which meant Dad had to exercise his manipulative control-freak tendencies long-distance, usually by calling Sawyer's brothers instead of him. "How are they doing?"

"Head of the Dalton Foundation is leaving. Frank Bolliver."

He rubbed his hand over his face. "That's how they're doing?"

"Dad thinks since you're out of a job, you might want to consider taking this one."

The old resentment leaped up, fresh and shiny new every time. "I'll give that tons of thought."

Finn chuckled. "Just the messenger."

"Last week it was Tom telling me Dad's golf buddy needed a partner in his firm. He doesn't let up, huh."

"In his own misguided way he's trying to help. He thinks you're lost at the moment."

"What do you think?"

"Not my job to comment, man, but if you ask me, you're spiraling downward big-time."

"That's what I thought." Sawyer stood, went to the window, peered out through the single pane at kids riding sleek narrow scooters down the block. "You ever wish you'd done something with your music?"

"Come on, bud. There's a time when you have to lose the rock-star dreams and grow up."

"Right." He laughed to himself for the idiotic impulse of sharing himself with his own brother. That wasn't how the Kerns operated. "I'll work on that."

"Whoops, gotta answer this e-mail. *Some* of us still work for a living. I'll let you know what I hear about Phil."

"Yeah, have fun with that." Sawyer tossed the phone on his bed in disgust. Sometimes he wondered how he was born into this family.

He trudged toward the bathroom to scrub off anything left of his hangover and to brush his teeth. Three steps into the hardwood hallway, he tripped over a colorful plastic toy and had to jam his hand on the wall to keep from falling. In the distance one of his nephews screeched in fury, another burst into loud tears, accompanied by yips from the dog Skittles, and yells of, "Shut up, Bobby, Uncle Sawyer's still asleep."

And there you had it. Episodes like this were why, during a painting session at Habitat for Humanity, when Melanie started talking about inviting "Fast Freddie" to be her room-mate because she wanted to support his struggles to stay clean, Sawyer had told an immediate white lie and said he heard Freddie hooked up with an old girlfriend, but that Sawyer desperately needed a place to stay.

Maybe Freddie really had given up his meth addiction, but Sawyer wouldn't bet on it. He didn't like the idea of Melanie alone with a guy who could be wired out of his mind and reason at any time. Not counting last night, Sawyer's mind and reason kept pretty close company. He'd be better for a naive idealist like Melanie. In fact, when he met her, he'd toyed with the idea that he could be *very* good for her, until his attraction faded naturally into brotherly affection. She was too childlike, emotions riding too close to the surface. Her sister…well, Sawyer would like to date her, but only if she stayed asleep the whole time.

A startling shout close by, seven-year-old Sam and six-year-old Jacob burst around the corner, aiming invisible weaponry. "Bew! Bew! You're dead from our laser guns!"

Sawyer clutched his chest and slumped obligingly against the wall. He knew about being shot, stabbed and otherwise relegated to dead-body status, having grown up with three older brothers. Even their dog, Dante, had been male. Another reason uptight, permanently outraged women were such a mystery to him. Seemed like they managed to complicate the simplest things—like Alana going ballistic in the face of a misunderstanding. Which was why he always dated women who were calm, in control, unshakeable in the face of chaos, like his mother. Or like his brother Mark's wife, Maria, mother of the fearsome foursome taking over his house, while Mark tried to find the family new digs abroad. Maria could simultaneously carry on a conversation in the middle of a full-blown good-guy/bad-guy war, cook dinner and fold laundry without missing a beat.

Sawyer grinned at the kids, who were vigorously debating whether or not plasma slime was fatal to aliens, then went into the bathroom to find pain reliever for his headache, which had just gotten worse. Outside the door more yells, then feet pounding down the hallway accompanied by scrabbling paws and shrill barking, more noise than an assortment of sixty-pounders should be able to make. Sawyer grimaced and downed some extra-strength acetaminophen. He'd go along with his plans to move in with Melanie today, even if Dragon Lady was still there, spreading protective wings over her sister. Apparently she thought Melanie was unable to take care of herself.

Which, now that he thought about it, was one thing they had in common.

He showered quickly, stepped over and around and through kids and a hyper dachshund to pack a couple of suitcases and box his laptop and CD player, some books and CDs. All of which he loaded into his beloved red Mistubishi Lancer, declining Maria's offer of help. She was busy in her enormous minivan, vacuuming the upholstery of crumbs and removing what looked like the contents of a McDonald's restaurant trash Dumpster. Apparently the kids had consumed their weight in chicken nuggets over the past two weeks; Maria was great about getting them out of the house so Sawyer could have a peaceful dinner once in a while. He'd noticed her having to shush the kids more often than he was sure she did at home, and had felt badly about the guilty apology in her brown eyes.

They could all relax once he moved out. Sawyer could handle Alana.

He said goodbye to the boys, not that they noticed, still deeply involved in the finer points of annihilating each other, hugged Maria and drove west across town into Wauwatosa, then Washington Heights and Betsy Ross Place, where he found himself on edge looking for Alana's silver Prius.

Still in the driveway. He expected to be disappointed and wasn't. In fact, he found himself strangely exhilarated, looking forward to the challenge of tangling with her again—figuratively, at least.

He used his key to go through the side door into the kitchen and called her name a few times. No answer. In the bathroom? In the shower? Out on a walk? He grabbed his suitcases from the car and hoisted them up the beautiful dark wood staircase to the second floor and into the room where he'd spent the previous night.

Alana's bag was still there. Which meant she still claimed the room Melanie said he could have because his large frame was more comfortable in a queen-size bed than one of the twins in the guest room.

More conflict. He'd do the gentlemanly thing and offer to sleep in the guest room, but it made more sense for him not to have to change rooms after she left.

He supposed if he tossed her things across the hall now, she'd pitch a fit that would deafen him.

"Oh. Um. Hi. Sawyer."

Alana. He spun around, prepared for battle…and found himself reacting to her not as the shrieking shrew, but the way he'd reacted to her asleep in his bed. Her eyes were wide, anxious but not hostile. She looked slightly unsure of herself. Her rich, dark brown hair was damp—yes, she'd been in the shower—and curled gently around her face; he remembered its fragrance. She wore jeans and a clingy peach-colored sweater that reminded him forcefully of what lay underneath.

What was the point of that thought? She wasn't merely not his type, she was his antitype.

"I, uh…" She looked down at his suitcases. "I thought maybe you'd changed your mind about living here."

"*Hoped* I'd changed my mind?"

"Oh." She laughed shortly. "No, of course not."

"Liar." He winked, thinking maybe he could charm her into not being a pain in his…move-in.

No acknowledgment of his humor. "I guess we got off to a…weird start."

"I guess we did. Not all bad, though." This time he managed a we-had-some-serious-fun smile.

Nothing.

She gestured to his suitcases. "You're still planning to live with Melanie."

Hadn't they just settled that? He'd try humor one more time, then he was going to get annoyed. "Oh, no. Those hold my drug, alcohol and condom supply. I'm never without them."

No response. He sighed. "Yes, I'm still moving in. I need this place."

"So…" She sent him a direct, challenging stare. She'd make a great middle-school teacher. Or cop. Or judge, jury and executioner. "What happened at your old place? Why can't you live there anymore?"

He folded his arms across his chest. *Nobody expects The Alanish Inquisition.* "It got too crowded."

"Lots of roommates?" He saw the suspicion and disapproval in her eyes. *This guy can't even afford one eighth of an apartment.* What a piece of work. She was probably picturing drugs, orgies and animal sacrifices. What in their identical upbringing could cause Melanie to trust too much and Alana not enough? He was more curious than he should be.

"No, it was the kids." The boy in him who'd found ways to torment his brothers during the years he lacked their strength decided to see how far he could push before she was on to him. "Once you hit four, it gets pretty noisy."

Her eyes shot open. "You left your children? *Four* of them?"

"Oh, they're not mine. I'm living with my brother's wife. I'm *pretty* sure the kids are his. Most of them anyway."

She sputtered. "You…he…she…"

"So when I met Melanie and she had this place available, I jumped at the chance to ditch them all. I needed the quiet."

"I see." Her outrage was at full pitch. How could she swallow all this obvious bull, but refuse to acknowledge any truths he told her early this morning? "What…do you do?"

Sawyer shrugged. "Not much of anything these days. Just kind of casting my net around, enjoying a break."

"Well. That must be…freeing."

"Yeah, you know, sleeping late, doing whatever I want all day."

"But you're able to help my sister with the expenses of living here?" Tight lips, rigid body, frosty, frosty disapproval.

Sawyer would shiver, but he'd heated into truly brilliant creativity. "I can always hit up some of the rich, married women I service if I need cash."

"You—"

"Alana." He took a step toward her, hand held up. Enough.

"What?" She spoke through her teeth.

"This is ridiculous."

"What do you mean?"

"I'm kidding about the married women. And my brother Mark was transferred to Germany; he's there finding his family a house. Maria and the boys needed a place to stay because their place in Menomonee Falls sold sooner than they expected, so I said they could stay with me."

"For God's sake." She lifted her chin. "You made it sound like—"

"You'd already decided I'm bad news. I was curious how bad. Apparently impressively bad."

"Melanie said to give you another chance. I was trying."

"By assuming I'm a jerk?"

"You acted like one."

"Okay." He took another step toward her. He wanted to see her eyes, watch her face change. And, yes, he was a man, to enjoy the rest of her up closer. He never got to hold her gorgeous body against him the way he planned when he woke to her a second time. "So can we start over? Without preconceptions?"

"Well. I guess." Her color rose; she took a step back. "If you'll stop lying."

Grrrrr.

"I'll do my best." He held out his hand. "I'm Sawyer Kern, Melanie's roommate."

Her grip was reluctant. "Alana Hawthorne, Melanie's sister."

"Nice to meet you." Their hands lingered, then separated. He had no idea what to say to her now. They'd been together an entire night, argued like an old married couple; it seemed wrong to pretend they were just-met strangers. "Uh, so this is your room?"

"Since I was ten."

He looked around. Decorated with the sweet femininity of a butch drill sergeant.

"Melanie took out my personal stuff. I guess to get it ready for you."

Oops. Apparently he'd jumped to judge her, too. "How long are you staying?"

She smiled with all the warmth of a nurse proffering a bedpan. "Until I'm sure you're not taking advantage of my sister."

He wanted to laugh. He'd moved in to *protect* her sister. "I'm not interested in doing that. Just in escaping four boys and a dog's worth of chaos. When they leave, I go back home, Melanie's fortune, house and honor intact."

"I know I seem overprotective, but her track record with men is…" She pressed her lips together. "Anyway, I just wanted to meet you before I move to Florida."

At least she was loyal to her sister. That was one good quality he could focus on, to keep himself from strangling her… or something else, which he wished he could stop wanting to do. "I'll sleep in the guest room while you're here."

"Oh, well that's very nice of—"

"Unless—" he gestured to the bed "—you'd like to share again?"

Her hands went back to her hips. Her brows dropped as if they had weights.

"No?" He gave her his best charmer grin. Did she have no sense of humor? "Out of luck for a repeat, huh?"

"Completely." She held herself as if she'd had her vertebrae fused. The challenge was irresistible.

"So…no chance even for a quickie right now?"

Her eyes darkened. Her fists were going to crack her hip bones if she wasn't careful. "If you keep harassing me like this, I'm going to—"

"Tell on me?" He took another prowling step toward her. He was being a complete jerk, but she thought he was one anyway, and he was tired of trying to be nice. Something about her made him edgy and angry and excited and horny all at once. Didn't he say he usually went for calm women? He should go downstairs right now, move the rest of his stuff up into the guest room and act like a saint so she'd trust him with her sister and leave.

And he'd never get to touch her again.

Another step. She glanced to one side, glanced back. Glanced to the other. Glanced back. Her lips parted.

Where was the outrage now? Swamped by hormones? Was he affecting her the same way she was affecting him?

Or did she just get off on guys who were jerks?

Sheesh. If he wasn't getting more and more turned on by her, he'd be feeling contempt. He'd be thinking women like her were why nice, non-caveman guys couldn't get a break.

Unfortunately, now that he was one step away from her, his inner caveman was acting up. He could see the sexy indentation at the base of her throat, her collarbones peeking from her scoop neckline, the shadow of cleavage—and no, he wasn't just looking down her shirt because he had also noticed her eyes were wide and anxious again.

Worse, her proximity brought back details of his predawn sexual raid in startling clarity. The way she'd arched and moaned, the way her hips undulated with his rhythm, the way—

"What are you doing?" Her voice came out a cracking whisper. She didn't step back or move away; her eyes held his. Where was Ms. Dragon Lady now?

"I'm…" What *was* he doing? "…going to kiss you."

His words snapped her out of whatever human form she'd taken. *"What?"*

He winced. Did she have to make so much noise? "Did you not hear?"

"I heard fine. Now, you listen to me." She had the gall to thrust a finger at him, as if he were nine and she was his den leader. "You're here living with my sister, and you are *absolutely* not allowed to take any advantage of— Mmph."

Kissing her was the most polite way he could think of to shut her up. Certainly the most appealing.

Her lips were warm and clung to his, and what was supposed to be a single me-man, you-woman kiss turned longer.

His hands moved, one over soft hair to rest behind her head, one over soft fabric to press her curving body against him.

He'd just learned something. Calm women, the kinds he liked, the kinds he'd always dated, were calm when they kissed, too. Not this set-me-on-fire passion. He broke the kiss for a second, then went right back in, not able to get enough.

Surprisingly strong arms shoved him back. Startled, he let go and immediately regretted it.

"You—you—you…" Outrage again. But she hadn't moved a step away from him. Not even half a step. Ms. Dragon Lady talked a good chaste game, but wanted to be ravished. He wanted to roll his eyes. His type of woman was straightforward, honest, no games. "That is *absolutely* beyond anything I've ever— Mmph."

He'd learned something else. It was easier to keep kissing her than stand there and be lectured. Given that her shrieking seemed always at the ready, he might have to do a lot of kissing this morning.

Except the more he kissed her, the more he wanted to do a lot more than kiss her, and the more it annoyed him on behalf of nice guys the world over that she responded to him when he behaved like a caveman and shrieked at him when he was polite.

This time the arms were even more surprisingly strong, and once she'd pried him off her, she actually took a step back, then another, then folded those strong arms across her heaving chest, face flushed. She finally meant business.

"Stop. Just stop."

"About time." The muttered words came out louder than he intended. Her eyes widened and for a second she looked hurt and he felt like a toad even if she did deserve it. But the moment of vulnerability clicked off in a second and her mouth opened for more screaming. He hurried to cut her off—with words this time. "I meant that you seem to enjoy being... coerced."

That didn't help, either. Around women like her he needed to learn not to say whatever was in his head.

"I'm just going to tell you one thing. You are not staying in this house and I'm going to do everything in my power to bring Melanie to Florida with me, out of your depraved company."

Depraved company? Did she stay home and read Gothic novels all day? Now he was frustrated, horny and completely disgusted. "That was two things."

"What?"

"You said you were going to tell me one. You told me two."

"How can you possibly pick on that after—"

"Because you refuse to listen or—"

"—you *kiss* me, when—"

"—let me finish my sentences."

"—you and Melanie are dating seriously."

He frowned. Had he heard that correctly? "What?"

"See?" She tossed her thick below-shoulder hair scornfully. "It doesn't even occur to you that it's a bad idea to come on to your girlfriend's sister?"

"Huh?" She had him at a complete loss. Again. Women were the most mysterious beings on the planet. "Melanie and *me?*"

"She's had enough pain in her life being betrayed and tossed around by men. Give her a break. Just pack up and leave before you hurt her."

Okay. A small lightbulb, just a small one. "Your sister and I are not—"

"Come on, Sawyer."

"No, listen to me, Alana." He went to grab her arm and she sidestepped him. "Just stand there and listen. We are not dating, not seriously, not casually, not at all, nothing. We've never…ever. Not even half—not even a *sixteenth* of what you and I did."

Her blush came back. "Why should I believe you?"

"Uh…" He pretended to think it over. "Because I'm telling the truth?"

"Melanie said you were the guy for her. The One."

"The *who?*" Was there something that happened to women in childhood that turned them into total aliens? *Would* plasma slime work on them? He needed to consult with his nephews.

"So excuse me if I don't trust you. At all. You seem like a pretty typical Melanie choice."

He thought of Fast Freddie. "I take it that's not a compliment."

She shook her head, but sadly. Whatever else, she did love her sister.

"Think about it, Alana. If Melanie and I are dating seriously, why aren't we sleeping together?"

"I don't know. You snore?" She wrinkled her nose at his skeptical look. "Okay, maybe not that. But—"

"Alana." He held up his hands and, by some miracle, she fell silent. "I swear to you. Your sister and I are not dating. I don't know why she told you that. Here's another tidbit for your truth file. Melanie planned to ask someone else who works at Habitat for Humanity to move in with her. A dubiously rehabbed meth addict known as Fast Freddie, who makes 'speedy delivery' jokes and has a facial tic and questionable hygiene. I thought I'd make a better roommate, so I stepped in."

She closed her eyes. "Oh, God."

"What?"

"That sounds like something Mel would do."

Wow. She actually believed him. A miracle. "So are we straight here?"

She frowned, but did seem derailed from her total condemnation of Sawyer—and why did he care? "I'll have to talk to Melanie."

"That's fine."

"And it doesn't change the fact that you...did what you did to me last night when I was asleep."

He shook his head. Why bother even trying? "Yeah, that was because of my unfortunate drug habit. You'll be glad to know you could have been a rock and I still would have gone for you. Probably would have woken up all bent out of shape, though."

"Oh!" Her face grew pink with fury, then what he said must have hit her, and she burst out in an actual giggle.

He grinned and her face grew pinker. "However, today, an unusual day, I have not yet injected, ingested or inhaled any foreign or illegal mind-altering substances, and I have to say I prefer you to any rock I've ever met."

She snorted again, but something shifted between them.

"Truce?" He held out his hand.

"Well..." She took it and gave him a firm shake. "For Melanie's sake."

"Good."

"But stay away from me."

He smiled into her eyes and watched her pupils darken and dilate. He hadn't let go of her hand yet, and she hadn't pulled hers away.

He had the distinct impression that she wanted him to stay away from her exactly as much as he did.

5

ALANA POURED Comet onto a green scouring pad and went at the white porcelain sink as if she were training for the Olympic scrubbing team. Her life had been peaceful and calm for a long time. Moving to Chicago had been a huge upheaval, but the subsequent six years, once she settled in, had been rewarding and enriching. She'd met Sam when his sink backed up and she surprised him by being the one who showed up to fix it. Their friendship had proceeded slowly and naturally into romance. She'd made other friends in the building, at her gym and book group, and enjoyed an active social life. Chicago had provided plenty of culture. Life had been good.

Even her breakup with Sam, though difficult for him and guilt-laden for her, hadn't put her through too much devastation, which validated her decision not to marry him. Mostly a matter of breaking habits and coping with sadness and regret. Though if Alana had still been involved with him, she might not have found it as practical to plan a new life in Florida.

She rinsed the sink, stared critically and shook in more Comet. Now her life was in transition again, so it was not too surprising that she was a little—okay, maybe a lot—stressed. The nagging restlessness in her relationship that came to a head when Sam proposed, and the same in her job during this past year after they broke up had been unsettling. Gran's fall had been even more unsettling, especially having to guess at the details—Gran claimed minor injuries to one leg, but she'd say that if she shattered every bone—then all the exhausting planning and packing for the move, then Melanie's meltdown and now…

She scrubbed harder.

Sawyer.

He was the most infuriating, funny, charming, infuriating, sex-y, sex-ual, sex-ist *infuriating* man she'd ever met.

Did she mention infuriating?

More Comet, more scrubbing. There were gray streaks on the bottom of the sink where pans had rubbed, and stains, probably coffee or tea, maybe something tomato-ey. All of them were doomed.

If Alana's apartment showed dirt or clutter, it was a guarantee that she was relaxed and happy. When you-know-what hit the fan, she cleaned. Even when she was little, if Mom hadn't come home when she said she would, if she'd had one of her bad days, one of her wild days, brought yet another man home, Alana would tidy the house, arrange her toys, make her bed and Melanie's, drag out the vacuum cleaner and the full array of cleaning products seldom touched by their mother, and she'd subjugate her pain and fear to creating cleanliness and order.

Which was why this sink would blind users by the time she was done. Because second only to Sawyer's unforgivable behavior yesterday morning had been hers. She didn't know what had disabled her common sense, but while her brain had been extremely clear about staying away from him for Melanie's sake, and for the sake of female pride everywhere, her body had entirely other thoughts. Alana had acted like the worst type of no-means-yes woman, something she'd never done in her life, not even in high school when hormones and

inexperience could easily cause that conflict to tip the wrong
way.

Not Alana. She'd said no with ruthless sincerity to junior-
year boyfriend Jake and senior-year boyfriend Ted no matter how crazily her lust was acting up. In college she'd said
yes, but only to Alan, and only after an appropriate amount
of dating time. After college, she and Sam had proceeded
with degrees of intimacy appropriate to their deepening relationship.

Yesterday morning? With that man who lied and teased and
came on to her completely inappropriately? She'd acted like
a seventeen-year-old virgin, still into movie-star fantasies of
men, who is faced with her first real one. Attracted, repelled,
wanting, knowing she couldn't have. Or shouldn't. On edge
like she'd never been before, excited, shooting sparks, so out
of her mind that she fell, splat, victim to his magnetism and
hadn't cared. Had. Not. Cared! Since when had she not cared
about moral issues? Since never. Since she had a mother who
didn't. And now a sister who didn't. Someone in their little
family had to, and that had always been Alana.

At least she'd stopped at kissing Sawyer, though my God,
the man could redefine kissing.

Alana chose a new spot on the sink, ignoring the light sweat
spreading on her body that didn't have enough to do with
the exertion of cleaning and too much to do with the heated
memories.

Were he and Melanie an item or not? Not that it mattered.
Alana was staying away from Sawyer no matter what. Or at
least she was going to make sure she tried a hell of a lot harder
than she had yesterday. No means no means no! She'd practice
if she had to.

But if they weren't dating, then Melanie lied saying they
were a couple, which would hurt. She and Alana saw eye to
eye on very little, but Alana had always trusted her to be honest. For so many years, they had only each other.

Alana would have to ask. Melanie hadn't come home after work yesterday, which she often didn't, and Alana was in bed by the time she made it back, so Alana hadn't been able to—or been willing to, given that the day had been confusing, to say the least—confront her sister. The second Melanie came downstairs this morning, assuming Sawyer wasn't around, Alana was going to pounce and not let go until she got the truth from *somebody* around here.

She went to work on the metal drain stopper, determined to make it sparkle again. Today she'd try to sort this all out so she could make definite plans to move on. She should make sure to call Gran and Grandad later to check on Gran and keep them up-to-date.

"G'morning." Melanie bounced in, wide-spaced hazel eyes bleary with sleep, her blond hair a ratty mess around her head, wearing only a wrinkled pink Bratz T-shirt that barely covered the necessities. She looked absolutely adorable.

"Morning, Mel. Sleep well?"

"Mmm." Melanie started a huge yawn, then bit it off. "God, Alana, what are you doing?"

"There was all this…stuff staining the sink, and I thought I'd help…"

Melanie rolled her eyes and pulled open the refrigerator, which could use a scrub, too, now that Alana looked. Something purple had dripped down the front, and there were dried bits of green—lettuce?—on the bottom that could use wiping.

Uh-oh. She was really upset. But as long as she didn't start wanting to wash windows, she was sane. If the glass cleaner came out, it was time to call in professional help.

"You ever stop to think that all your efforts here might seem like a criticism of the way I live?"

Temper flared. Alana lobbed the scouring pad into the sink. "You're welcome."

Melanie got out the plastic jug of orange juice and let it thud unnecessarily hard on the counter where they ate.

Alana took a deep breath. This was not how she wanted their sisterly interaction to start this morning. Or any morning. They couldn't seem to help setting each other off. Which was most of the reason Alana had moved away to Chicago.

"Sorry, Mel. I'm cranky. And you know me, cranky equals cleaning."

"I knew that. I shouldn't have taken it personally." She poured herself juice, sloshing a bit and of course not wiping it up. "What's going on?"

Alana cleared her throat, and then realized in an odd flashback, that was what their mother had done before she approached a difficult subject. In a Pavlovian response, Melanie's hand carrying the juice glass froze halfway to her mouth.

"Uh, I had a kind of strange talk with Sawyer yesterday."

The orange juice glass lowered. The sleepy green-brown eyes turned cautious. "Yeah?"

"He says you're not dating." Alana made sure her voice was gentle, no accusation implied. "That you're not involved at all."

Melanie's glass hit the counter with a sharp crack. She mumbled something.

"What?"

"I said not involved *yet*."

"But…I mean…has he shown any interest?" She held her breath, shocked at how desperately she hoped Melanie would say no.

"He's the kind of guy you always told me I should want. And I do. I finally found a good one."

Alana nodded carefully. What she was walking on would make eggshells feel like bricks. Melanie hadn't answered her question directly. If Sawyer had shown interest, she'd lose no time throwing that fact in Alana's face. Which meant when he'd come on to Alana, he was single. She wasn't going to take that thought any further just yet. "Why didn't you tell me the truth?"

"I did. I told you I'd found the guy I'd like to spend the rest of my life with. That's the truth."

Alana felt a twitch of irritation at the hair-splitting. And a traitorous kick of jealousy she was ashamed of. "You didn't think I'd assume you were together already?"

"I didn't think you'd come barreling up here to check my story before we'd had the chance to get to know each other."

"Okay." Alana gave in, moistened a sponge and wiped up the juice spill in front of her sister, not looking at her in case she was rolling her eyes again. "You said you'd known him a solid month. I thought that meant—"

"I didn't say solid."

Alana turned back to the sink, rinsed the sponge, picked up the scouring pad and went to work again on grout turned brown with mold. Otherwise she was going to want to smack her sister. "Okay. You probably didn't say 'solid.' So maybe you didn't lie and I'm sorry if I accused you. But you certainly misled me. On purpose. How come, Mel?"

Her sister sighed, but not in exasperation. "Because I was excited about meeting him and jumped the gun…as usual. Because I thought you'd feel better about moving to Florida if you thought I was settled with a good guy, which I finally have a chance to be, with Sawyer. Because you worry about me and everyone more than you worry about yourself and I wanted you to take a break, at least on my behalf."

Alana turned and met her sister's eyes across the kitchen. "Is that really why?"

She shrugged and grinned lopsidedly. "I care about you, too, you know."

"Aw, Mel." Alana swallowed hard. "Thank you."

"Am I the only reason you're cleaning? When you start on grout, it usually means something more serious."

"Oh. That. Well." How could she tell Melanie Mr. Dream Guy made another pass at her? That Alana had responded? She couldn't. More to the point, she didn't need to, because that was over, done with, not going to happen again. "I was confused about you and Sawyer. And, yes, worried. You know me."

"Don't worry. He is remarkable. Really. Did you know he's Dalton Brewing?" She grinned triumphantly at Alana's shock. "Uh-huh. Sawyer is a direct descendant through his mom, though his dad was no slacker, either. Big-shot CEO. Major cash in the family."

Alana stared stupidly. Sawyer, the consummate player bum, came from money? "Why didn't you tell me this before?"

Melanie grimaced. "I had some adolescent idea that I wanted you to trust me no matter who the guy was."

"Aw, Mel…"

"I know. I have to earn the trust. And I will. You'll see."

Alana murmured encouragement, feeling uneasy. She hated hearing her sister talk about her as if she were an ogre parent. But maybe she acted like one. She'd certainly felt often enough as if she had to be one. "Is that why neither of you is worried about the 'between jobs' thing?"

"Yup. He doesn't need a job to begin with." Melanie fished a cottony piece of white bread out of a plastic bag and dropped it into the toaster. "You should see his house in Whitefish Bay. Only a block from the lake and about a bajillion bedrooms."

"Ah." Alana smiled weakly, feeling sick. She'd treated him like a loser down to his last dollar.

No, wait, he'd acted like one.

Why?

She rinsed the now bright-white sink and dried her hands. The answer was obvious. And painful. Because she'd assumed. Judged. Jumped to conclusions about his character and motivations. And in return for that favor, he'd played her like a banjo.

Ouch.

"He was a successful lawyer, but had health issues, so he chucked it." Melanie grabbed the barely browned piece of toast from the toaster and smeared it with sweetened peanut butter, leaving the crumb and peanut-butter gobbed knife sticking out of the jar. "He promised himself he'd take six months off to rest, then start on something less driven. I guess his dad and brothers are all workaholics and Sawyer felt like he was turning into all of them."

"Oh." What else could she say? Money didn't guarantee good character, but this man wasn't who she thought she'd met. Lawyer meant graduate degree. Most of Melanie's boyfriends thought junior year of high school was plenty of education. Her sister would have it made if her plans went through and she and Sawyer ended up together. Not that money was the most important thing, but security…she and Melanie would never, ever take that for granted, even after so many safe, good years with Gran and Grandad.

"Sawyer has three older brothers, Finn, Tom and Mark." Melanie bit into the toast, crunched happily, looking excited and starry-eyed. "Guess what author his dad was into?"

"Huck Finn, Tom Sawyer, Mark Twain." Alana drank the last of her coffee and decided she'd better eat something to settle her churning stomach. Not peanut butter and tissue paper-white bread. "Do you have any bran cereal?"

"Do I *look* like someone who has bran cereal?" Melanie pretended to be insulted. "You want prune juice, too, granny? Guess what. Don't have that, either."

Alana stalked to the cereal cabinet. She liked high-fiber breakfasts because she stayed full longer and had less trouble keeping her weight in check. She wasn't like Melanie who could eat sticks of butter all day long dipped in chocolate batter and deep-fried and not gain an ounce.

"Lucky Charms? Cocoa Puffs?" She stared in exaggerated horror, pushed boxes aside. "Oh, thank God, Raisin Bran."

"Raisin Bran?" Melanie frowned, mouth full of peanut butter. "Better check the expiration."

"December of this year. It's fresh." Alana got down a blue-rimmed bowl, pulled open a drawer for a familiar spoon. It felt good being in this house again; it felt like home. "Maybe one of your old boyfriends was a closet bran-eater."

"Maybe." She shrugged as if she thought it extremely unlikely. "So when are you leaving?"

"Want me out of the way before you jump Sawyer, huh." The joke came out more bitterly than she'd intended; she dumped too much cereal in her bowl and had to put some back. She knew she was intruding on Melanie's life, but her sister's impatience to get rid of her hurt.

"No, I know you're anxious to get to Florida, and since you get now that Sawyer is not my usual guy—"

"You want me out as soon as possible."

"No! I want to make sure we have dinner at a new restaurant—new to you—on North Avenue that I think you'd like." Melanie laughed ruefully. "Will we *ever* be able to communicate normally?"

"Probably not." She crossed the kitchen and gave Melanie a long hug. "You and me?"

The phrase was one they'd used often when their mother was out of the house or out of commission. Melanie squeezed her, then let go. "You and me."

"What, I'm not invited?"

"Hey, Sawyer!" Melanie's face lit up. "How was your second night?"

"Better than the first. And also not as good." He winked at Alana, who immediately turned to pour herself another cup of coffee, though more stimulation was the last thing she needed. He wore a loose T-shirt and khaki shorts, bare feet, his dark hair tousled appealingly; he moved with a lumbering swagger that was so masculine her mouth was practically watering.

Melanie laughed as if she'd never heard anything so clever

in her life, though she obviously didn't get the joke or she wouldn't have found it funny.

"Good morning, Alana."

"Hi there." She tossed the greeting over her shoulder, safe by the coffeemaker. "Glad you slept well."

"Did you?"

"Sure." Not. Even with her new sleeping pill—but not the second one this time—she'd had a hard time dropping off, lying in the bed she'd slept alone in for over a decade. One night with Sawyer and it was as if he belonged there with her. She wished she'd taken the guest room after all.

"So what's on the calendar today, roomies? Looks like Alana got a jump on the cleaning." He started opening cabinets. "Mugs here? Whoa, someone likes candles."

"We ate by candlelight all winter. Gran said it chased away the gloom of early darkness. She bought them by the case. Mugs are here." Melanie got down a Green Bay Packers mug for him, apparently unconcerned to be caught wearing only a shirt, which lifted and clung sexily when she reached into the cabinet, though Sawyer didn't seem to notice. Er, not that Alana had meant to check for his reaction.

Sigh. Sometimes, Alana wished she was more like her sister. Not very often. But if Sawyer had come down while she was half-naked, she'd have turned beet-red and run from the room to put on sweatpants.

"Alana cleans when she's upset."

"Oh?" He moved next to her—too close, she felt her whole body wanting to lean into his tall strength—and poured himself a cup of coffee. "You upset?"

"No. No." She inched away, sat at the kitchen counter and sent Melanie a look of death behind his back. "I'm fine."

"Good to hear. Can you pass the Raisin Bran?"

"What?" Melanie jumped to get him a bowl. "You like Raisin Bran, too?"

"I have it every morning. Creature of habit."

"Then this is your box." Alana knew there had to be some reason Melanie had healthy cereal in her cabinet. "I'm sorry, I had no idea—"

"I think I can spare you a bowl of Raisin Bran." He grinned and took the box, sat on the stool next to her across from Melanie, to Alana's intense but not altogether unpleasant discomfort. "Especially after what I put you through."

"Oh. Well." Dammit, she was blushing again. "That's… it's… I don't—"

"So what are you doing today, Sawyer?" Melanie had the slightest edge to her bright tone. "I promised Edgar—he's my coworker—that I'd shop with him for a surprise for his girlfriend's birthday, then I'm at Habitat for Humanity this afternoon. You coming?"

"Yes, after lunch. I'm going to stay close to home this morning. Get settled in. What about you, Alana?" He got milk from the fridge and handed it to her; she tried not to notice how easy it was for him to hold the full gallon at arm's length. Oh, what she'd missed by being asleep that first night, and not being able to see or experience fully what—

"Milk?"

Oh, help, she was still staring. He'd asked her something else, too.

"I…don't really…I should get going…Florida." She shook her head at the milk, completely disgusted. Could she not even come up with a complete sentence?

"Stay another day. I don't think I've convinced you I'm a good guy yet." He took the milk jug back. "I'll take you both out to dinner tonight."

"You don't have to—"

"Sawyer, that is *so* sweet." Melanie reached across the counter and squeezed his forearm, then rubbed up and down before she let go. "We accept."

"Um, I guess one more day." If Alana could survive the next twenty-four hours remembering the touch of this man's lips while watching her sister fling herself at him. If Sawyer was everything Melanie said, and if Alana could be convinced he wasn't also a player, he really would be great for Melanie. Better than anyone Alana could have imagined her sister ending up with.

She'd just stay in Florida the rest of her life.

"Gah, what time is it?" Melanie peered at the digital clock on the microwave. "Yikes. I'm meeting Edgar downtown in half an hour. Gotta go shower."

She crammed peanut butter and toast into her mouth and grabbed her coffee to take upstairs, her legs flashing strong and muscular under the pink T-shirt.

Alana put her sister's plate in the dishwasher, then went back to her Raisin Bran, eating quickly so she could also go upstairs and not be alone with this guy she didn't know how to feel about anymore.

"How are you doing today, Alana?"

"Oh, I'm fine. Thanks." She swallowed a mouthful. "Melanie's been telling me about you."

His eyes turned wary. "Good things?"

"Yes." She frowned. "Why, is there something bad?"

Sawyer laughed and shook his head. "You don't let down your guard, do you?"

"Sorry. I'm still not over that first, um, encounter."

"Mmm." He held up a hand, put down his coffee. "I talked to my brother again this morning. Police are involved. My drink had been laced with…ready for this?"

"I think so."

"Benzodiazepine. Also known as the date-rape drug."

"Who would want to date rape you?"

He jerked his gaze to hers. "Is that an insult?"

"No! I was just—" She rolled her eyes when she realized he was kidding. He had her off-balance all the time. The feeling was unfamiliar and vulnerable. And challenging. And a little exciting. "Go on."

"The culprit was the jealous ex-boyfriend of a woman, Debbie, who I was, uh, talking to."

She shot him a glance. "You mean, trying to hook up with."

"Me?" He put his hand solemnly to his heart, looking so innocent she had to smile. "The upshot is, when I climbed into bed with you, Alana, I had no idea what I was doing."

A snort of laughter came to her lips before she could suppress it. As far as she was concerned, he knew what he was doing better than any man she'd ever been with.

"Something's funny?"

"No, nothing."

"Come on, something."

"Sawyer…"

He nudged her shoulder with his. "Tell me."

"Fine. The part where you said you had no idea what you were doing…" Blush, blush, mumble, mumble, why did she have to be either dorky or hysterical around this man?

"My God, was that a compliment? From you?"

"Don't let it go to your head." She blushed harder when his eyebrow quirked. "And no puns on that one, either."

He grinned, and she found herself smiling back, which felt suddenly natural and uncomplicated, a first where they were concerned.

Maybe he was telling the truth. Maybe he had been all along. "Apparently I owe you an apology."

"Yeah?"

"For assuming you were like all the other guys Melanie has brought into her life. Since she was about fourteen."

"Sounds like enough of a record that you felt comfortable making snap judgments."

"They'd always worked before."

"And then I fell right into the stereotype that first night."

"Yeah, kind of." She ate another bite of cereal, then put the spoon down. "One thing…"

"Ye-e-es?"

"You said you remember what happened. Between us. That night."

"Ohh, yes."

Her body reacted as if he'd touched her. His voice was so...

Steady, Alana. "You really thought I was someone else?"

"Uh, yeah." He sighed deeply, though she could tell he was still enjoying himself. She wondered if he ever didn't. He seemed like the kind of man who grabbed life by the glass half-full and hung on. Probably not hard to do when you were born into stability and got to stay there. "I remember nothing after leaving the party. When I came to in bed with you, it was dark. I assumed you were the woman I'd been talking to at the party. She'd been very...friendly."

Alana sent him a look of schoolmarm disapproval which made him chuckle, which made her feel as if she'd won the lottery.

"I put pieces together and decided I'd brought her—i.e., *you*—home and that we'd been at it all night, I just didn't remember." His voice dropped lower. "Given how good you looked and felt next to me, I wanted to make sure there'd be something I *would* remember."

"Oh...I see." She really needed to concentrate on Raisin Bran or she'd turn into mush and pour onto the floor.

"But when I couldn't wake you up, it seemed selfish and vaguely perverted to satisfy myself, so I just—"

"Yes, I know."

"And now..." He grinned wickedly. "You owe me."

"What?" She stopped melting instantly, stiffened in her chair. "You can't be serious."

"Alana."

He'd gotten her. Again. Once more, she was walking the

Sawyer tightrope, always about to fall off one side or the other. "Right. You were kidding."

"I'm sorry." He gave her an unbearably sexy sidelong look. "I've been teasing you too much. But it's been a long time since anyone thought I was trouble and it's kind of fun."

"For you, maybe."

"C'mon, you're not loving every minute of your time with me?"

She was, that was the problem. "I have decided you're an okay guy."

"Something in particular tipped you off?"

"Melanie promises you've been telling the truth. And I can sort of piece together what you said and make sense of it. And she said you...can afford to live here."

He moved uncomfortably. "Oh. Yeah. That."

"You didn't want me to know?"

"It's more fun when people don't."

"Why?"

"Assumptions." The playful look was fading from his face. "Those snap judgments you love so much."

She nodded, slid off the stool and took her unfinished cereal to the sink, afraid she was about to discover he was such a good guy that he didn't want to be associated with the immediately—though shallowly—appealing aspects of wealth and power, that he wanted people to judge him for who he was, not what he had or represented.

Sawyer Kern was starting to seem too good to be true. Not in a choir-boy way, not at all, because he had that mischievous sense of humor and bad-boy sexuality spicing up what appeared to be solid character. Maybe even depth. A fabulous and rare combination.

Which meant he *was* perfect for Melanie.

Which meant the only thing Alana would accomplish by staying was to get in the way of her sister's happiness.

6

"WHERE ARE YOU taking me?" Melanie followed Edgar down Water Street in the Third Ward, an area of old factories and warehouses reclaimed and reinvented as shops, theaters and restaurants. They'd passed the galleries and funky furniture stores, and were headed, as far as she could tell, for the Milwaukee River. Just before they reached the bridge, Edgar stopped in front of one last small building on the west side of the street which housed a wig shop.

"You're buying Emma a *wig* for her birthday?"

He gave her a look and opened a door to the left of the store which led into the foyer for the building's upstairs residents.

"I thought we were shopping."

"We are."

"In someone's apartment?"

"Why not?"

Her frown turned into surprise when he pulled a key from his pocket and unlocked the security door. "You live here?"

"Yup."

"We're going to your apartment?"

"Nope."

"Edgar, why are you being so mysterious?"

He waggled his thick eyebrows, smirking at her impatience,

and led the way up the worn-carpeted stairs. "All will be re-
vealed in time."

"Honestly." She followed, thumping up each step to signal
her pretend displeasure, all the while brimming with excited
curiosity. She'd never thought of Edgar as either mysterious
or romantic. Wouldn't that be something if he turned out to
be both? The day was looking better and better after the tension with Alana over breakfast. Melanie had been late leaving
the house, as usual, but hadn't passed any cops speeding east
on I94, and found a miracle parking place only a few yards
from where she'd promised to meet Edgar. Good luck always
needed celebrating, at very least with a good mood.

"Here." Edgar stopped outside the scuffed door marked 2B
and rapped with the scratched knocker. A deep voice answered
unintelligibly, but Edgar must have decided that was permis-
sion enough because he pushed open the door and gestured
Melanie in ahead of him.

Three steps into the apartment she could see this was the
home of an extraordinary artist. All four walls were hung
with bright abstract paintings, great smears of colors with
black squiggly lines dancing through them; they made her
feel cheerful and somber all at once. On every surface sat
sculptures, thin black metal bodies contorted in various sexual
pairings, some tender, some gymnastic, some nearly violent,
all erotic. Simple figures, but tremendous movement and passion in each coupling.

By the doorway to what must be a bedroom, two chairs
had been set opposite each other, a board laid between them,
covered with a sheet splatted here and there with gold paint.
On the sheet, lovingly arranged, was jewelry.

Melanie walked toward it, mesmerized. Was this what
Edgar had in mind for Emma? Earrings, bracelets, necklaces,
all in silver, her favorite, twisted in delicate spirals, looped in
playful circles or zigzags, adorned here and there with gems
in rich colors that caught the light spilling through one of the

windows. An artist's eye had set them here to be displayed to their advantage.

She hardly knew where to look first. Such talent. Such beauty. "All of this, the paintings, the sculptures, the jewelry…"

"One guy. He's good, huh?"

"Good?" She turned to Edgar, overcome. "He's a genius."

"I had a feeling you'd like it."

"Why?"

"Because it's exuberant and colorful. And sensu—beautiful. Like you."

"Edgar." She smacked him on the arm to cover her pleasure and astonishment. Pleasure at his nice words, though he complimented her often even though they'd been friends for two years now—he was sweet that way. Astonishment because she figured he'd invited her along shopping this morning because he had no confidence in his taste. Given the way he dressed, Melanie would have agreed. She expected they'd hit the mall jewelry store, he'd go straight for some chunky tasteless disaster, and she'd have to steer him away from his instincts to protect poor Emma from every woman's nightmare.

But this…

How could he have such an eye for beauty and leave the house looking the way he did every day? Today's ensemble: lemon-yellow stained shirt and horrible dull green pants— don't get her started.

"I'll be right out." The deep voice originated in the rooms beyond the jewelry. "Have a look around."

"That's Sledge."

"Sledge? As in hammer?"

"He's the artist. My neighbor. I live upstairs, bumped into him a couple of times and we got friendly. He's a good guy."

"He's brilliant." She finally managed to calm down enough

to concentrate on the jewelry pieces singularly. A necklace in the middle caught her eye, a gorgeous piece that made her lust to own act up. She needed to remember this was not her purchase. "Tell me more about Emma's taste. You said she's—"

"Pick out whatever you'd want. You and she are similar. Whatever you love she would, too."

"You're sure?"

"Yeah." He shoved his hands into his baggy pants. "Yeah, I'm sure. If I think she'd hate what you choose, I'll let you know. But I doubt it."

"I don't see how you could hate any of this." She gazed at the assortment, pretending to consider, though the necklace was smiling at her. *Take me. You know you want to.* "I like this one…"

Edgar lifted it, a series of silver circles, some perfect, some slightly twisted, with jewels of varying size and color attached around the circumferences, apparently randomly. Except the balance, the color, the energy of the piece made her sure there was nothing random about it.

"Try it." Edgar opened the clasp, held out the necklace. Melanie turned and moved her hair out of the way, thinking Edgar had really nice hands, neat with strong-looking fingers. He needed to take that much care of his fashion sense and that horrible helmet of hair…

The weight of the necklace settled onto her collarbone; she felt him brush the back of her neck, then the cool metal fell against her skin. She touched the silver rings where they lay neatly arranged across her chest, a perfect length to show off a low-cut sweater or to accentuate a high one.

"Well?" She turned back to let Edgar see.

He nodded. He was looking at her with a weird intensity, undoubtedly imagining Emma in the necklace. "It's beautiful."

The emotion in his low voice surprised her. As did a funny

wistful ache in her heart. He adored Emma. Wasn't that what every girl wanted? Melanie hoped the woman knew how lucky she was. "If Emma is anything like me, she'll love it."

"She's a little like you." He hadn't taken his eyes off her. There was tension in the air, nothing that had ever been between them before, and she didn't like it. Edgar was always so easy to be around. Was something wrong?

"Hey, sorry guys, I'm just out of the shower. Had a phone call this morning and everything got pushed back."

Melanie whirled toward the sexy voice and immediately fell in love. Deeply. Irrevocably. As quickly and thoroughly as she'd fallen for his necklace. Long, brown, curling hair, dark and damp from the shower, the color high in his high cheekbones, gray eyes dancing between long lashes. Earrings in his ear, loop in his nose, body by Michelangelo. Oh, how she lusted.

Which meant this guy was bad news. She could type him without hearing another word. He was fabulous in bed, as talented as he was artistically. Passionate, articulate, a dynamic and challenging partner. And self-absorbed to the point where if you weren't right in front of him, or under him, you didn't exist. How often had she dated this guy in one form or another?

Too many times. But, oh, he was beautiful.

Why couldn't she fall this hard this quickly for Sawyer? Maybe real love took time and she was already on her way. She sure as hell hoped so.

"Melanie, this is Sledge. Sledge, Melanie, my coworker."

"Ah, so this is Melanie." He took her hand and held it without shaking, looking deeply into her eyes. *Take me. You know you want to.*

No. She wouldn't go there. She knew where she'd end up— yesterday's girl, sitting by the phone, feeling like a stomped-on chewing-gum wrapper. She deserved better. She deserved a man like Sawyer who would carry part of his woman's heart in his own all day and all night. He still spoke respectfully and affectionately about his old girlfriends.

Melanie spoke about her exes with homicidal rage.

"Nice to meet you." She managed to withdraw her hand, feeling as if she were pulling off a body part. "I *love* your work."

"That necklace looks like it was made for you."

"It's for Edgar's girlfriend."

Argh. She was an idiot, making sure Sledge knew *she* wasn't Edgar's girlfriend. If they were friends, he knew already. Worse, a guy like him would know exactly why she'd rushed to let him know.

He grinned and Melanie was lost. His eyes crinkled at the corner, his teeth were white and straight, and he radiated easy joy. He raised his fist and touched it to Edgar's. "Emma will love it. It'll look great with all that gorgeous black hair."

"Yeah. Yeah." Beside her Edgar had stiffened and looked uncomfortable. What was up with him? He couldn't possibly be jealous of Sledge's compliment. Emma had the good sense to fall for Edgar; she wouldn't let someone like Sledge onto her radar.

"I'm just sayin'…" Sledge lifted his palms in surrender.

"Sure. I know. She'll love it. I'll take it."

"Sweet. It's yours. May I?" He reached toward Melanie's throat, and Melanie, who had no such good sense and whose radar was picking up every signal Sledge sent, knew that if he touched her she'd burst into flames right there and char her favorite orange top. But oh, baby, did she ever want him to.

"I got it." Edgar stepped behind her; the necklace pulled up then fell away. She missed it immediately.

"Thanks." She glanced at Sledge who was watching her intently, lips curled in a knowing, predatory smile. He wanted her. He knew she knew it. She needed to get out of here. *Now.* "We ready?"

"Sure." Edgar handed the necklace to Sledge, who slid it onto a piece of waiting tissue paper and wrapped it. "Can I pick it up later? I don't have the cash now."

"No problem. Thanks for stopping by." He aimed a sultry wink at Melanie that further weakened her already weak knees. She'd have to take Edgar's arm to make it out the door.

"It was a pleasure." She grabbed Edgar and started dragging him toward the exit.

"Wait." Sledge leaped, catlike, over to a bookshelf studded with those suggestive sculptures, which she didn't want to look at in the same frame with him, and came back with a business card. "In case you need to get in touch with me, Melanie... for any reason."

She took the card, determined to play this cool. "Oh, thanks."

"Anytime." He gave her another lazy smile. "Just call."

"Sure." She managed to pull herself away from his tractor-beam gaze and grin. Out in the hallway, she fled down the stairs and emerged into the warm sunshine of summer, feeling like a bunny that had just escaped from a mountain lion. She was so stirred up, she wasn't even going to beg a peek at Edgar's apartment, which of course she'd been dying to see.

First garbage can on the street, she was tossing his card.

"Thanks for coming, Mel. The necklace is just right."

"No problem. Emma will love it."

"I know she will. Do you want to...get a coffee or something? Early lunch?"

"Oh, thanks, sweetie. I need to get home."

"To Sawyer."

He sounded so snarky she turned and stared. "Well, yeah. How am I supposed to fall in love with him if we don't spend any time together?"

He shook his head, those startling blue eyes filling with

sudden humor. "Good luck with that. And thanks again for coming."

Sure. She reached on tiptoe to kiss his cheek. "Mmm, Edgar, you smell divine. Whatever that is, keep it on for Emma tonight."

"Will do." He turned abruptly and strode down the sidewalk back toward his building. Something was odd about him today. She couldn't tell what. She'd ask him Monday, make sure he was okay. She couldn't bear to think of anything troubling him. If Emma ever broke his heart, Melanie would rip hers out, barehanded.

A deep breath and she headed for her car, got in, started the engine and buckled, still a little shaky from her encounter with Mr. Heartbreak Waiting To Happen. Then ta-da, through her windshield she saw the prize: a garbage can, mounted on a streetlight. Perfect. She'd get out *right now* and throw the damn card away, because if she didn't, she'd be taking it home with her, and she did not want his name and number anywhere near her house, which had a phone in it. And a bed.

She held up the card, still clenched in her hand—Sledge Bolton, Artist—then shamed herself by pressing it to her nose and inhaling the faint scent of his apartment. Even that tiny hint of him made the card seem too precious to throw out.

Come on, Melanie. She was being ridiculous in precisely the way she'd promised herself not to be ridiculous anymore.

Seat belt undone, she was about to pull the door handle, when a car honked impatiently behind her, someone anxious for his own miracle parking space. She craned her neck and saw a line of cars behind the honker, waiting for him, waiting for *her* to get out of the way.

Oh, crap.

She tossed the card onto the passenger's seat, buckled again and backed out in a hurry.

There was nothing magical about that trash can. She had plenty at home. First thing through her door, she'd march into the kitchen and throw his card away. No, she'd tear it up first, then throw it away. Or even better, put it through the shredder so she wouldn't change her mind and try to piece it back together.

There. That was her plan. The New Melanie would follow through and be rid of The Temptation of Sledge Bolton in less than half an hour.

7

ALANA NEARLY JUMPED out of Sawyer's car. The three of them, Sawyer, Alana and Melanie, had eaten a very good dinner at Il Mito on North Avenue, a small, cozy neighborhood restaurant, new to the area since Alana had lived here and indicative of how the restaurant scene in Milwaukee had become more sophisticated in the six years she'd been gone.

However. What should have been a nice, relaxed celebration of her last night was anything but. Melanie had been hyper and spent the evening trying to get Sawyer to flirt with her. Sawyer had been polite to Melanie, but spent the evening trying to get Alana to talk to him. Alana had avoided Sawyer by spending the evening trying to get Melanie to reminisce with her. And so it went, from the excellent salads to the fresh and unusual pasta and pizza dishes, to the deliciously rich desserts. As soon as Sawyer paid the check, the three of them had practically sprinted for the exit and jumped into Sawyer's Mitsubishi for the silent drive home.

In the humid summer air, Alana opened their back door, aware of Melanie and Sawyer hovering behind her. Thank God she was going to Florida in the morning; she should have showed more backbone and started her trip today. The thought of leaving Milwaukee again hurt and, okay, she'd miss the thrill of Sawyer's attention, but she couldn't take much more of this weird triangle. Melanie deserved a guy like Sawyer, was clearly smitten with him, and Alana needed to be out of the way for them to discover if anything could ignite between them.

Inside, she flipped on the kitchen light, tossed her purse on the counter and glanced at her watch. Not late, but with the time difference too late to call Gran and Grandad. She'd left a message earlier telling them she planned to start her drive the next morning, Sunday. A hurricane watch was in effect for Central Florida; Cynthia was expected to land Tuesday morning. Alana should be there in case they hadn't taken proper precautions and needed her help.

"Any messages?" Melanie hurried to the machine on the counter by the refrigerator. "Yes! One!"

"Maybe Gran and Grandad." Alana watched Melanie curiously. She sounded awfully excited about a phone message. "Are you expecting a call?"

"More like dreading one." She put on a big show of rolling her eyes, then whirled around and jabbed the button. "Might as well check."

Uh-oh. Alana's alarm bells started ringing. This was classic Melanie man-behavior.

"If that's 'dread,' I'd hate to see 'eagerness.'" The murmur came just over Alana's head, private and intimate.

"Hmm." Alana turned to smile coolly, which didn't work because Sawyer was standing close, one hand up on the cabinet above her, and with wine from dinner still in her system, it was hard to do or feel anything but…hot. "I'm not sure she's—"

"It's Gran." Clearly disappointed, Melanie turned up the machine and Gran's quiet voice again filled the kitchen she'd spent so many hours in for so many years.

"…but don't come down until this storm is over, Alana. We'll be fine. There's still a chance the worst will miss us to the north, which will make more of your trip more dangerous. Even if it hits here, we have friends who've already helped us secure the house and will drive us to the evacuation shelter at the high school. We aren't taking any risks and don't want you to, either, for your sake and because we'll worry. Love you, girls. Grandad says hi and sends his love, too. Goodbye."

Melanie deleted the message, frowning at Alana. "What are you going to do? If you leave tomorrow you'll get there right when Cynthia hits on Tuesday."

"I'll have to drive in two days instead of three."

Melanie nodded, chewing on a fingernail. "That would do it."

"Two ten-hour days driving by yourself?" Sawyer shook his head. "That's crazy. Plus there's plenty of bad weather ahead of the actual landfall."

"It wouldn't be *that* bad." Melanie was clearly not pleased to be argued with. "And she'd be there to help Gran and Grandad."

"They already have help." Sawyer spoke calmly, gesturing to the machine. "Your grandmother said so. Why should Alana put herself in danger?"

"She wouldn't." Melanie fisted her hands on her hips. "She'd be safe at the shelter with them."

"They'll worry about her driving all that way."

"Not if they don't know she's driving until she shows up."

"Stop." Alana covered her ears. The more rational Sawyer sounded, the more shrill Melanie got. *"I'll* decide. It's my neck, and they're my grandparents."

"Hey." Melanie jabbed a thumb into her chest. "They're mine, too."

"Melanie, for heaven's sake, you know what I meant."

"Okay, okay." Sawyer backed to the kitchen door, hands up in surrender. "If you two are going to start shrieking, I'm going upstairs. Hate to miss a word, but…"

"Sorry, Sawyer." Melanie deflated sweetly. "Sorry, Alana."

"S'okay, Melanie." Alana rushed to make peace. "We're all tense about the storm."

"Yeah, don't worry about it, Mel." Sawyer's cell rang. He fumbled in his jean's pocket and hauled it out. "Hello...yes... Oh, right. Hi, Debbie."

Alana peeked at Melanie to see her reaction at the same time Melanie peeked at her. Then both shrugged comically, which made them both cover their mouths to keep from giggling.

"Thanks. Yeah, um, I enjoyed meeting you, too."

Alana lifted her eyebrows. Melanie mouthed, *I'll bet.*

Sawyer rolled his eyes and turned his back on both of them, which started the giggling again. His fault they were listening, because his large and magnificent body was blocking the exit.

"Tomorrow..." His voice dropped. "I'm free then, yes."

The giggles stopped. Melanie suddenly found her lack of manicure fascinating. Alana examined the floor for traces of dirt. Of course there wasn't any because she'd cleaned like a maniac all day.

She wasn't going to be jealous. If Sawyer wanted to go out with this—

Her eyes jerked to his broad back. Wait! *Debbie?* The woman he'd been trying to pick up at the party? The woman he mistook Alana for that night? In *bed?*

She was going to be jealous.

"Okay, see you then." He clicked off the phone and turned, glancing first at Alana, then at Melanie. "Well."

"Ah."

"So..."

"I didn't thank you for dinner, Sawyer." Melanie launched herself at him for a long hug, ostensibly to prove Debbie had a lower priority than she did. Alana quietly left the room to avoid watching the lingering full-frontal contact and trudged upstairs carrying even more jealousy, which she needed to dump out the window. Melanie, Debbie, Sawyer... She had more important things to do than moon over a man she wouldn't know much longer. Like decide what to do about her trip.

There was no point staying here any longer. Sawyer was exactly what Melanie needed, and Alana needed to be in Florida to help Gran and Grandad through the hurricane. But to avoid heavy traffic in the Chicago area she couldn't leave too early, and that would cut down the miles she could cover tomorrow, not a good thing if she planned to make the drive in two days. She didn't want to arrive too late Monday or, God forbid, have to spend another night on the road and show up only hours ahead of Cynthia.

But wait. She stopped in front of her room door. Another option which would solve traffic *and* timing problems was to get up after a few hours of sleep and leave tonight. She'd stoke herself up with coffee, get more than halfway to Florida by tomorrow evening, then to Orlando by Monday afternoon, in plenty of time to help prepare for Cynthia and ride out the storm. Leaving silently would ensure no awkward goodbyes with Sawyer. Melanie wouldn't object. She'd be relieved to be rid of her sister, at least on some level.

The house phone rang. Alana started into Melanie's room to answer Betty Boop when Melanie's voice rang clearly all the way from downstairs, too bright and too loud. "Oh! Hi. Um. Wow! Hi. Hang on."

Footsteps, running upstairs. Melanie, flushed and agitated, giving Alana a distracted and guilty smile as she passed into her bedroom, closing the door firmly, practically in Alana's face.

Was that the "dreaded" phone call? Alana's stomach turned sick with instinct. More man trouble? With Sawyer right here under her nose?

Alana shouldn't jump to conclusions, especially not again so soon. Melanie said she'd changed. Maybe she really had.

She trudged into her room and packed her bag, feeling sick and hollow. Sick with nagging uncertainly over her sister's behavior, but also because she was packing to leave Milwaukee again. Before dinner, over drinks at the Firefly Café, they'd run into Lucy Vola, a friend of Alana's from high school who'd shared Alana's passion for photography, and who hadn't sold out to practicality in her career but had a studio on North Avenue with her business-partner boyfriend.

Seeing her and having a lengthy catch-up chat about the business and about mutual friends and acquaintances reminded Alana not only of her disappointed hopes of a career in photography, but also of all the roots she'd put down here, the small-community feeling of Wauwatosa and the larger city. "Small-waukee," some people called it.

But she supposed it was normal to be anxious about moving. Starting over would be hard anywhere. And she could do better about keeping photography as a hobby once she was in Florida. Somehow she'd let that side of her slip when she moved to Chicago.

She undressed, grumpy and ill at ease, and pulled on her camisole and girl boxers. No sleeping pill tonight, not when she'd be getting up again so soon, which meant she'd sleep badly. Especially if she started thinking—okay, she was already thinking it—about how tomorrow night this would be Sawyer's room again, and he'd sleep in the bed she was about to climb into. Would he think about her? Every night? For weeks or only a few days? Would Melanie sneak in one night and claim her new territory, replacing their drugged, indistinct memories with vividly erotic new ones?

Probably. And when she did, Alana was going to be the dutiful saintly sister and be happy for her.

She slipped out into the hall and toward the bathroom, doubled back abruptly to get a shirt or other cover-up, then rolled her eyes and turned back again. Sawyer was still downstairs. He wouldn't—

The bathroom door swung open.

Not downstairs. Here. Tall and masculine, looking her over thoroughly. "What a nice bedtime surprise."

Oh, God. Alana took a step back, as if distance would make her outfit more conservative, and folded her arms over her chest. "I thought you were downstairs."

"I'm not."

Right. Just because she hadn't heard him clumping up, yelling, "I'm coming up the stairs now, make sure you're decent," she assumed the coast was clear? She was definitely not firing on all cylinders. Too much on her mind.

"Need the bathroom?"

She stared at his feet for lack of anywhere else she could bear to look, and tried to gather her exploded wits. "Uh. Yeah. Thanks."

"How much?"

Her gaze shot up. "What?"

"How much do you need to use it?" His eyes sparked mischief. "What's it worth to you?"

"Sawyer…"

"Because I think I might charge a small fee to get out of the way. With you looking like that—" he took a step toward her "—I'm not sure I can let you off easily. I might have to—"

Melanie's door flew open; she burst out, then froze at the sight of her sister in underwear and Sawyer standing very close to her. "Oh. Um. Hi, guys."

Alana felt her face turn hot. "I'm about to use the bathroom."

"Well." Melanie nodded rapidly, her expression strangely distant. "That sounds great."

Sawyer looked incredulous. "It does?"

It did? "Mel, are you okay?"

"Huh?" Her gaze snapped into focus. "Oh, sure. Yeah, fine."

"That phone call…?"

"A friend." She sounded exasperated. "Nothing you need to worry about."

Alana refused to let the dart hit. "Right. I know. Okay. You just seem a little—"

"I'm *fine.*"

"Good to hear, Mel." Sawyer shrugged at Alana and shook his head nearly imperceptibly. "Alana and I were just standing here discussing her need to—"

"Stop." She pushed past him, and threw a firm "good night" out the door before she closed it.

In the bathroom her eyes were bright and wide, her face flushed. She looked alive, slightly manic, but…pretty. She hadn't looked like that in a long time. In fact, she'd started to think her bloom of youth was on its way out prematurely.

Not today.

Oh, brother. She really did not need to have this big of a crush on Sawyer. Damn good thing she was leaving, even if it didn't feel good all the time. At any rate, she wouldn't see him again, so there was no point thinking about him further. If that was possible.

In five minutes, she'd taken care of her bedtime routine and stepped out again into the hall.

Where Sawyer waited, toothbrush in hand, having changed into sexy soft-looking shorts and a T-shirt which hugged his shoulders, skimmed his chest and fell loose around his waist.

"You're quick."

"Oh. Thank you. Or whatever." She was *not* going to blush again. Nor was she going to hesitate in the hallway any longer and gaze her fill of him. She was going into her room and closing the door.

C'mon, feet, move.

She managed it, closed the door behind her and breathed a huge sigh of relief. *This* would be the last time she'd see him. Nothing had changed. She'd sleep, get up, leave a note for Melanie and go. Then she'd call from the road and apologize for leaving without an appropriate farewell. Melanie wouldn't care. Both of them hated goodbyes anyway, because the ones they'd said to their mother had been so uncertain. When would they see her again? The next day? The day after? Not for a week? Never? So not comforting for little girls to have to wonder.

In bed, as predicted, Alana couldn't sleep. Every possible worry crawled out of whatever shallow crack had partly concealed it during the day and tormented her. Worry over Melanie, over Gran's health, tension over the long drive, even worry over all her furniture and belongings being trucked down toward the storm.

And, yes, about Sawyer.

The longer she tossed and turned, the closer the clock crept to the hour she'd decided to get up, the less she realized she'd sleep and the more agitated she became.

Honestly.

Finally, she felt her body relax as exhaustion took over. She could survive. Just a few hours of sleep...just a few...

It was time to get up. Her alarm was beeping, but she couldn't get to it. Couldn't make herself move. Someone was here in the room with her. Sawyer, taking her picture over and over again, then climbing into bed with her. Why couldn't she wake up? She hadn't taken a pill this time. She needed to wake up before his tongue and fingers and hands made her surrender again, before she fell so in love with him that she couldn't leave at all.

No, Sawyer. Stop.

He didn't, surrounded her with his body, undressed her, touched her everywhere. He was clothed, then naked, his chest hot against her, his thighs insistently parting her legs.

No, no, no.

He chuckled softly. *No means yes when you're with me.*

Then he was inside her, and her body caught fire from the inside out while his stayed cool and solid, urging her upward toward a climax that hovered just out of her reach.

In Florida, Gran and Grandad were trapped by a fallen tree, calling for her, calling while she was in bed with the man of her dreams.

I love you, Alana. Stay with me. I can't live without—

Alana woke up, breathless with panic, wildly aroused... and alone.

"Oh my God." She rose to her elbows, pushed her damp hair back from her face. Or more appropriately, "Oh, *thank* God."

Just a dream. Sawyer wasn't with her. Gran and Grandad were safe. Alana had time to get to them and make sure they stayed that way, though with her shaky and sick from not enough sleep, the drive loomed impossibly long and lonely ahead of her. A crazy undertaking.

Why had she dreamed Sawyer was in love with her?

More crazy. And crazier still to feel warm and blissful and cared-for and desirable when her dream thought he did.

She laughed to illustrate how gosh-darn wacky it was, but something in her heart refused to smirk along and the laughter never quite convinced her.

Did she mention crazy?

She dragged her eyes to the clock. Three-thirty. She'd planned to get up at four, might as well cut her losses and do it now.

Yawning, she stumbled to the bathroom, not thinking about Sawyer standing there hours earlier, not thinking about his warm body in the dream, not thinking about being unaccountably sad leaving him, not thinking about him, not thinking, not, not, not.

She showered, shivering from lack of sleep, towel-dried

her hair, then threw the towel sleepily around her and went back out into the hallway.

"Hi."

She couldn't believe it. She absolutely could not believe it. Had he been *listening* for her? Had he somehow known he could find her damp and naked except for draped terry cloth?

"What are *you* doing up?" she whispered.

"I couldn't sleep. You?"

"I'm...me, neither."

"So you thought a shower would help?"

Alana sighed. "I figured I'd just leave now."

"Sneaking out, huh?" He took a step toward her as he had earlier, but this time darkness made the wide hallway seem even more intimate, and this time Alana doubted Melanie would burst out of her room to interrupt; she was a reliable and heavy sleeper.

So this time Alana had to deal with him all by herself, and rely on her common sense and her strength and—

"Mmm, you smell good."

"Um. Well." She backed up. "Strawberry shampoo. Could you not stand so close?"

"Why?" He was barely making tone, but the silence in the house was so profound his voice traveled easily.

"Because...you're too close." She edged toward her room, hugging the wall at her back.

He followed. "Too close for what?"

Too close for sanity. "For rules of personal space."

"Answer this for me, Alana."

She frowned, not liking the note of intimacy that had crept into his voice. "What?"

"Do I make you as insane as you make me?"

Her breathing hit a speed bump. "I have no idea. I don't know how insane I make—"

"Completely…" He laid a finger on her bare shoulder, let it trail sensually down her arm.

No. He was *not* going to do this to her again. She was attracted to him, yes. So what. "Look, Sawyer, I'm on my way to Florida in about fifteen minutes, so there's no point in starting anything."

"We already started something. This is finishing. Or no, I don't like the sound of that. How about starting phase two?"

"Uh…no." To her delight, common sense gained ground against her dream and his magnetism. "My sister is nuts about you, you're going on a date tomorrow with Debbie, the woman you tried to pick up a few nights ago, but gee, who cares about any of that, how about a quickie with Alana while she's still here?"

"I never said anything about quick." He laughed at her glare, but without much humor. "Well, Alana, I'll say this, you sure know how to make a guy feel good."

Perfect. She was on a roll. "Sawyer, I am attracted to you, and the other night was really and very weirdly amazing, but…what's the point?"

"The point is that we can make each other feel good and I can distract you for a few extremely satisfying days until after the hurricane, because it's a dangerous decision to go now, a decision which will put an unfair burden of worry on your grandparents who already have plenty to worry about just taking care of themselves, which it sounds like they can do just fine without you, not to mention an unfair burden of worry on Melanie and…" He stopped for a breath and his gaze intensified. "On me."

She nearly growled. The last thing she wanted was for him to start making sense. "I need to be there."

"*You* need. This is about *you*. You can't stand your grandparents being there and you being here with danger approaching, because you love and want to protect them. I get that. I admire it. But putting yourself in the same danger isn't going to help them. They've been responsible, they've taken care of everything." His lips curved in a small smile. "They've even asked you not to make the trip so they don't have to worry."

She squeezed her eyes shut. *He* wasn't supposed to be winning with common sense. How the hell was she supposed to think this through clearly standing naked in a towel with him so close? Right now, she was afraid he could tell her she was descended from a family of Irish tree frogs and she'd believe him. "So you're going to distract me with sex?"

"I was planning to." He put his hands on the wall on either side of her head; she felt trapped by his body and wasn't sure she minded. "Until you graciously pointed out that I'm an unfeeling player who uses women indiscriminately to serve my body and my enormous ego. That what I feel for you is nothing special at all, that there isn't some extraordinary pull between us that defies logic and explanation. Right? Isn't that what you said?"

She had no idea what she'd said and less what to say now. He spoke in a low, even voice, but his words had the same impact as if he'd been shouting at her.

"Why are you so anxious to judge me badly? You take each shred of circumstantial evidence you can possibly use against me, then pump it up into an insurmountable character flaw." He lowered his face an inch from hers; she forced herself to focus on his chin, except even that was sexy to her. "What are you so afraid of?"

"I'm not afraid." Her hoarse whisper trembled. Her body followed suit. She was terrified, and she didn't know why.

"Then don't stop me. I dare you." His mouth found hers in a slow, gentle kiss that reached her so deeply it terrified her more. She pulled away. "Don't."

"Shh." He slid his hands up the wall, moved closer, kissed her forehead, her temple, her cheek. The only sound was her shallow breathing, catching with each touch of his lips.

She couldn't move, caught in the grip of exactly opposing forces, half instructing her to respond, half instructing her to break free.

"I have no romantic feelings for Melanie." He slid a warm hand under her hair, tipped her head back so she was forced to meet his dark eyes, serious under dark lashes, his features softened in the glow from the bathroom light which she'd been too startled to shut off. "I'm having coffee with Debbie tomorrow morning. Not exactly a hot date. After meeting you, I can barely remember what she looks like."

Alana lowered her eyes. Too much intensity, too powerful, too much temptation to believe him, believe everything, then take it further until she was expecting to live the dream she just had and believe he loved her. "Stop doing this."

"What, being right? Being sensible? Being made insane by you?"

"Yes."

He grinned. "I want you safe, Alana. And to prove that I'm not just out to get laid, I promise you that I will stay completely brotherly the rest of your time here, if that's a day, a week, a month or forever. Okay?"

She nodded dazedly, already feeling a sharp loss. "Okay."

"Good." He pushed away from the wall. "We have a deal. You stay until Cynthia's passed, and I act the perfect gentleman."

"Yes. Okay." She'd stay, not only because he asked her to, or bullied her into it, but because on some level she knew taking the trip now was madness. On some level she was grateful he reined in her blind obsession to do her duty and got her to acknowledge the right choice.

"Just one thing." He leaned in again.

She shrank back. "Oh, no."

"I'll keep my promise." A slow, wicked grin lit his face and melted a part of her she needed to stay solid and strong if she was going to make it intact through the next few days. "But there's nothing stopping you from inviting me to do whatever you want, however you want, whenever you want it."

8

SAWYER SHOWED UP at Alterra by the Lake coffeehouse for his morning date with Debbie slightly crabby. He'd been back home in Whitefish Bay in his workshop basement, locked safely away from the fearless nephew foursome, working on his new bedside table, today cutting pieces for the drawer. He wasn't the world's most gifted cabinetmaker, but he loved the work, the precision of measuring and cutting, the smell and feel of the wood, the satisfaction of working with his hands. He'd forgotten the way he could lose himself in the pleasure of the job. Why couldn't work be that way all the time? He couldn't remember once losing himself in the sensuous pleasure of writing briefs or researching precedents. And yet, he had no one to blame but himself in betraying his passion and marching like a child after the Pied Piper into a career that would please his family above himself. He was just lucky he got out before it killed him.

Some aspects of returning to regular full-time work appealed to him—he wasn't the type to be happy dithering around for the rest of his life—but losing the freedom to create wasn't one of them.

A woman carrying a whipped-cream-topped beverage bumped his arm. Not Debbie. Fifteen minutes earlier, he'd been absorbed in the work, totally unaware of time passing, a Bach CD playing in the background, when Maria called down asking him to move his car. One glance at his watch and he'd used language his discipline-happy father would have locked him in the garage for. Sawyer resented the interruption, wasn't looking forward to the date—Alana had blocked out any interest in Debbie—and he hated being late. Strike three.

Alterra was a Milwaukee institution. This café, Alterra by the Lake, situated, not surprisingly, across the street from Lake Michigan, inhabited an old flushing station for the city of Milwaukee waterworks. The pale brick interior, waterwheel and pump-room equipment were all original. In renovating, architects had made clever use of the existing space by providing two levels of seating—mezzanine and balcony—besides the first floor, where a cheerfully cluttered service counter offered Alterra's own coffees, teas, baked goods, breakfast items and sandwiches.

Another quick look around, half-afraid he wouldn't recognize Debbie since he'd been slightly out of his mind the night they met, Sawyer was relieved to see a familiar auburn head smiling from a table upstairs by the iron railing. He waved, pointed to the counter to show he'd be getting a drink, and ordered a plain black French Roast.

Up the stairs to the mezzanine level, most tables taken by students and adults chatting or glued to laptops, he climbed the next flight to the balcony seating which ran across the back of the building and gave an expansive view of the shop and the lake through the arched windows.

"Hi, Sawyer." She offered her hand and another smile, even warmer than the first.

Her fingers were cool, her grip firm, her yellow top low-cut, her black skirt short. Sawyer took the seat opposite, wishing he were still in his basement. Life was confusing enough right now. He'd convinced Alana to stay on a few more days for her safety, as well as for his own sake, and he didn't regret the pressure he'd put on her. But now that she was staying... should he bother trying to get closer when she'd be moving away in only a few days?

He didn't like that she'd had such a powerful impact on him in such a short time. Something was unnatural about this. *Obsession* was too strong a word. Infatuation? Something didn't feel right. Or at least nothing like any infatuation that had taken him over before.

"How are you feeling, Sawyer?"

He smiled, uneasy at the way Debbie lingered over his name. "Much better. How's Phil the human drugstore?"

"In trouble."

"With you?"

"With the Wauwatosa police since the party." She rolled her eyes. "With me, for weeks longer. We went out casually for a few months, but he started getting really intense and possessive and I broke it off."

"Smart move."

"He hasn't seen it that way. I met him on the rebound and should have known better." She shrugged, used her napkin to mop up a drop of spilled coffee. "I generally date a pretty laid-back type, because that's how I am."

"Ah." Sawyer, too, though he didn't want to say so and leave that connection hanging between them. If he'd met Debbie for coffee like this without having met Alana, he'd be excited at the prospect of getting to know this poised, beautiful woman. On the surface, she seemed much more his type. But Alana had his brain and heart in an illogical stranglehold.

Based on what? Maybe that was what bugged him. He'd had a few one-night stands with women he was attracted to superficially, but they'd never unsettled him like this. Women he liked on a deeper level he usually tried to get to know before they hit the bedroom. Alana occupied a nebulous middle ground. He was wildly attracted, but they'd never sat down and had a lengthy conversation. It was all chemistry between them, plus this odd challenge he felt around her, wanting to overcome her prickly resistance, to arouse in the clear light of day the passionate nature he glimpsed on the fog of that first night together, to get into her mind and find out what went on there.

They needed to relax one night in Melanie's kitchen with a bottle of wine. Or go out somewhere casually, without Melanie there to start the bickering. He might find out they were completely incompatible, which would make his life a lot easier when she left. If not...

He didn't want to think about *if not.*

"So I suppose you're wondering why I asked you out."

He blinked. Whoa. "Not to get to know me?"

"Oh." Debbie put down her coffee, which he noticed was straight up like his. He liked women who drank coffee the way coffee was meant to be, not clogged with fat and sugar and whatever other candyland stuff they did to it at places like this. He'd already noticed and approved that Alana liked hers black, too. "Yes, I'd like to get to know you, as well. I really enjoyed talking to you at the party, before you..."

"Did involuntary drugs?"

"Right. That." She laughed. She was beautiful, laughing, showing extra-white teeth, swinging extra-red hair.

He might as well have been gay for all it did for him. "Why *did* you invite me out?"

She leaned forward and put her clasped hands on the table, light brown eyes enhanced by mascara-thick lashes looking squarely into his. Direct and businesslike. He liked that in a woman, too. "I found out some very interesting things about you from Dan."

"Like?" He knew. How many times had he had this conversation? Most recently with Alana.

"Like that you're Dalton Brewery."

"Yeah." He sipped his coffee, but acid had already started

churning in his stomach and he didn't need more. Money again. Damn stuff. If it wasn't his family heritage and extremely convenient, he'd be tempted to get rid of it. But then, of course, it was easy for him to say; he'd always had plenty.

"And that the head of your foundation is leaving."

"Have you been talking to Finn?"

She smiled politely, clearly not about to be interrupted. "And that you have a lot more affinity with the arts than he did and could take the foundation in a different direction if you were in charge."

"Okay." He gritted his teeth. "What's your point?"

She lifted a hand. "Hear me out. It'll be worth it, I promise."

Sawyer straightened his legs abruptly under the table; his shins smacked the railing and he pulled them back, trying not to grimace. He definitely did not want to spend his morning being told what to do with his family's money. Attempted seduction, no, he wasn't in the mood, but at least that would have been exciting and flattering. His big old male ego was bruised already, and now Debbie turned out to be Dad Part Two. "I'll listen. But I'm not planning to take—"

"Just hear me."

He drew his hand impatiently down his face. "Yeah, okay."

"As I told you at the party, I work in insurance, but I'm also an artist, a painter. There are a lot of really talented people in this city."

"Right. I've been to some of the open gallery nights."

"Yes." She smiled, her eyes assessing him. "Those are great events. But I'm talking specifically about artists who show a lot of promise but might not have gotten to the gallery stage yet."

"What about them?" Sawyer resisted looking at his watch.

"I want the Dalton Foundation to buy me a building."

He laughed bitterly, took a sip of his coffee. "Good luck with that."

"There's one for sale in the Fifth Ward, the old Franklin Seed Company warehouse."

"Okay." He was both annoyed and impressed that she ignored his jabs and continued calmly. "What will you do with this building?"

"Turn it into studio space for young artists. Most can't afford to rent a place separate from where they live."

He thought of the guy Melanie had been babbling about over dinner at Il Mito, his tiny apartment crammed full of work that no one ever saw. "Why would they be able to afford this space?"

"We give it to them for next to nothing. A token amount and a share of the utilities. Then open it to the public at certain hours for a small fee so people can watch talent being shaped, watch works in progress. Periodically, I'm thinking four to six times a year, we invite Milwaukee's art-loving community for a dinner event and show, so wealthy investors can meet the artists, see their work and buy or commission new pieces, talk them up to their rich friends, their companies, etc. Essentially they'd become patrons."

"This isn't the type of thing the foundation invests in."

"You could change that. Let me tell you the story of one kid..." She told him about a young talented man catering a party for extra cash, who met an art-loving couple and struck up a friendship. The couple hosted a party for him at their lakeside mansion, and one of their friends loved his work so much, he had his company buy paintings for its lobbies throughout the country. "We want to make it possible for this to happen on a regular basis, instead of leaving it to fate."

Sawyer nodded, interested after all, at least somewhat. "Go on."

Another story, another artist's path to success through chance. Kids who didn't want to sell out by getting a corporate job, who deserved a chance doing what they loved; a student whose parents were so furious he wanted to paint for a living, they kicked him out of the house. Another woman who could only afford studio space in a bad neighborhood was mugged and raped.

Sawyer cringed, already feeling partly responsible. Debbie continued her well-planned pitch by painting her own picture—of a city young artists would be proud to call home, building on the success of the art museum's new addition, broadcasting Milwaukee to the country as more than sausage, beer, cheese… "And the Green Bay Packers."

He grinned. "Lest we forget."

She went on, Sawyer paying serious attention now, caught up in her glowing description of the ornate stone building, her vision of its renovation—skylights installed, large windows to look over the river and let in the light, different directions and intensities at different times of day. Green heating and cooling systems, making use of steam already piped under the city streets for heating, plants on the roof for natural cooling. Studios on each of the six floors, partitioned but open, so artists could communicate if they wanted, so visitors could see finished works displayed, as well as works in progress. "Introducing the public to affordable original artwork, and giving young people a chance to see some financial rewards for their talent and hard work."

To reel him in, since she'd already hooked him, she listed the other powerful local companies who had already pledged to invest. She and her partners had nearly reached their dollar goal before they announced the project publicly. The Dalton Foundation would be able to put them over the top if it agreed to be the largest donor so far.

"And not just painters, sculptors, photographers…" Her gaze turned sly. "Cabinetmakers, too."

He laughed. "You've definitely been talking to my brother."

"I'd never come to a meeting unprepared."

"Okay." He sipped his coffee, definitely interested, excited even, he admitted it, and certainly impressed. The project seemed to promise something personal to him, though he had no intention of working in a drafty old building next to twenty-year-olds throwing paint at canvas to express their angst. But to be in charge of the foundation as a way to help other kids not have to sell their souls—at least not until they gave what they loved a real shot—that would be a job he could get behind. "No promises, but send me a proposal and I'll look it over."

He'd do more than that, he'd do what his father wanted, for once gladly, and think seriously about taking the job, as long as he could give their grant-giving a different emphasis, away from energy and medical research, important as that was, and more toward the arts, making sure people who needed to keep creativity in their lives would be able to do so.

He and Debbie finished their coffee, chatting about other topics. As he suspected, they had a lot in common. In any other circumstance he'd find out if she was involved, and if not, ask for her number to see what they could start. Today he had no desire to. Maybe that drug Phil gave him scrambled his brain permanently.

Because as he waved goodbye to Debbie and headed back to his car, a crazy thought hit him. If he bought the building for Debbie, the building would need a manager.

And if he could find some way to get Alana the job, maybe she wouldn't leave Milwaukee.

9

ALANA TURNED another page of the photo album she'd pulled from a bookshelf in the living room and exclaimed again, laughing out loud at the picture of her and Melanie, ages twelve and ten, fighting in the backyard over the sprinkler on a hot day. She remembered that day, one of the few times she'd gotten the better of her younger sister. Grandad had taken the picture from the back steps moments before Alana wrested control of the weapon and chased Melanie all over the yard, soaking them both and beating the heat at the same time. Afterward, they'd come inside to freshly baked oatmeal cookies and lemonade with mint from Gran's garden. After growing up with Tricia for a mom, it had been like moving from an inner-city war zone into an episode of *Father Knows Best*.

Okay, she was exaggerating. Melanie would certainly say so, too, but Alana couldn't quite forgive their mother for her neglect, or at very least, her complete lack of understanding about anyone's needs but her own.

Another page turned, another picture, this one of their dog, Carver, a Cairn terrier mix, in the act of jumping for a ball Alana was holding out to him. By the blurry image and Alana's missing head, she'd guess Melanie took the picture.

"Knock-knock?"

Alana jumped and closed the album. "Sawyer."

"Did I startle you? Sorry." He was polishing an apple on his white Nike T-shirt, glancing at the book in her lap.

"I didn't hear you come in."

"Catlike tread." He took a big bite of the apple and grinned; her whole being responded to that smile. For God's sake.

"How was your coffee date with Debbie?" Acid showed through what she'd planned to be a casual tone. Oops.

"Fun." He came to the doorway of the living room and leaned an elbow up on the jamb, watching her intently. "But I'm not interested, and it turns out she isn't after me at all."

"Oh?" She opened the album again. Her attempt to sound disinterested hadn't worked, either; she sounded as if her heart had just started beating again.

"She's after my money."

"Oh, God." Alana wrinkled her nose in disgust even as she wilted into relief. Call her Pollyanna, but the whole idea of valuing someone for what he had instead of who he was repulsed her. "How romantic."

"It was okay, though." He examined the apple for another likely biting place. "I'll tell you about it sometime."

She nodded, turned a page pretending to examine a photograph carefully while minutely tuned in to his presence.

"Don't you want to know when?"

"What?" She looked up to find him chuckling, turning the apple around in his long fingers. "When what?"

"Dinner tonight? Drink? Both?"

She blinked, completely taken aback. "You and me?"

"Uh…" He pretended to look confused. "Is there someone else in the room?"

"Sawyer…" She hugged the album to her chest. "Thank you, but I don't think that's a good idea. I agreed to stay on during Cynthia, but it doesn't mean—"

"Melanie will be out tonight. She called me from work. I don't think there's much in the refrigerator, so I suggested going out." He crunched into the apple, which he'd nearly finished.

"I was going to go to the supermarket and—"

"Great, I'll come with you." He ate the last few bites, grinning with sneaky triumph. "You drive."

Alana couldn't help smiling. What a piece of work. She also couldn't help a silly burst of satisfaction at his insistence that she drive. Sam never let her except on long trips, a ridiculous male ego stunt. She remembered Gran telling her long ago before she could really understand—she was probably all of eleven—when she'd commented on Grandad helping in the kitchen wearing an apron, that it took more male security and strength not to worry about appearances than it did to cling to stereotypes of macho behavior. "Fine. We'll go. I'll drive."

"Hey, are those old pictures?" He gestured to the album. "Can I see?"

She nodded, strangely reluctant.

"I'll wash my hands." He disappeared toward the kitchen. Alana let her shoulders relax, realizing they'd been up somewhere around her ears. Why did this man set her so on edge? Maybe because she never knew what to expect next. Charm, teasing, seduction, friendship. He fascinated her, and tired her out, too. With Sam she always knew what to expect, right from the beginning. She'd never had such a smooth courtship. They drifted right into togetherness, each knowing it was what the other wanted, too. None of this agony of push-pull.

But also none of this excitement. Was this a tiny version of the danger and thrills Melanie seemed to want from men? Alana would go gray in six months at her level.

"Okay, clean and ready."

She held out the album but he crossed the room and sat next to her, close, so their hips nearly touched, his arm draped casually across the back of the couch behind her. He smelled of soap and Sawyer. Immediately, and predictably, her heart sped up, her shoulder wanted to lean into his. Had he implanted Alana-magnets under his skin?

"The first half of the album is mostly pictures Gran and Grandad took." She leafed through a few pages, conflicted, as if letting him into her past was like letting him into her life, which she guessed in a way it was. "This is Mom."

"Ah." He peered intently for a few seconds. "Melanie never talks about her. Where does she live?"

"This week? I don't know." She turned the page again, not wanting to go on about Tricia, hoping he wouldn't ask. "Our dog, Carver. Melanie and me. My first birthday party."

"You're a *lot* older than one…"

"I was ten. But it was my first party. Mom didn't go for that kind of thing. Here's our trip to Williamsburg, Virginia."

He watched with her, listened to her explanations, laughed at the stories, didn't press when she hurried past photos that pushed too many buttons. She felt warmed by his interest, cozy sitting with him here like this, in a truce, in a trance.

Why couldn't he fall for Melanie?

She nearly snorted out loud. Who was she kidding? Her heart would crack and shatter. She might as well admit a large part of the reason she was still here was that he asked her to stay.

"You said the first half of the album was pictures taken by your grandparents. What's the second half?"

"Oh. Pictures I took. I used to think I was a brilliant photographer." She laughed nervously, closed the book and glanced at her watch. "We should probably go to the supermarket if we want to—"

"Oh, no, you're not getting off that easily." He took the album gently from her, flipped halfway and started looking, turning pages, concentrating on each shot. She watched, trying to see the pictures through his eyes, fidgeting, painfully aware she was being judged. At the same time she was interested to see her own work again after such a long time. Gran and

Grandad kept this album here; Alana's originals were in some box she hadn't opened in years. She watched critically, page after page, seeing both the promise and the limitations.

Looking at the pictures now was like seeing an old friend and regretting having lost touch.

"Wow." He stopped on a shot she'd taken of the city just before dawn on a ridiculously cold winter morning from Bradford Beach, which jutted out into the lake north of the city. In the sky above, a half-moon pierced the blackness. Her flash caught mist rising from the lake, and the first suggestion of dawn had turned the downtown buildings into glowing orange-pink rectangles. "This is stunning."

"It was very, very cold. Minus ten or so. I was completely crazy to be out in it. But, yeah, I love the shot."

"Alana, this is incredible." He flipped a few more pages, then turned to face her, his features serious and thoughtful. "You are talented. A real artist."

The flood of pleasure at his praise surprised her. "Thank you. I haven't taken any pictures in years."

"Why not?"

Alana shrugged, trying to remember when her passion had started cooling. "It wasn't like one defining moment when I gave it up. More like a gradual waning. There was no money in the type of photos I wanted to take. I had a busy job—I don't know. Seems if I were really cut out for it, I wouldn't have been able to stop. Maybe I should start again, just for fun."

"You should." He touched her knee, which made her want him to touch her again. And again. "I'll tell you why I'm so sure you should, since you're sitting there thinking it's easy for me to say."

She lifted an eyebrow.

"I wanted to be a cabinetmaker in high school, but in our family it was understood you'd get a high-paying, high-status job. I took a fairly wimpy stand, then folded and went to law school, became a lawyer. Once in a while I'd uncover my tools, do some work, but unless you can keep at it, it's not satisfying. Or that's what I told myself. Sometimes I think now I was punishing myself as thoroughly as possible."

Alana held her breath, thinking of how often she'd had the urge to take her camera out and how often she'd come up with reasons why she couldn't. All of which seemed so crazy now. Had she been punishing herself, too?

"Then when I had to quit my job six months ago, I took it up again. Now I have no idea how or why I chose to live without the satisfaction working with wood gives me. It feeds my soul, I guess. Without some form of creative self-expression, life is pretty barren."

His words jolted her. She knew exactly what he meant, and an odd sense of joy bloomed in her chest. She did miss the sometimes frustrating hunt for the perfect shot, the rare excitement in capturing precisely what she wanted in a frame, those precious times when she hit it—color, light, composition, all perfect. "That's it exactly. Yes."

"I'm guessing your soul is hungry these days?"

She nodded, holding his gaze, feeling the tension between them, not sexual this time but something deeper, some connection through absolute understanding. "I hadn't even noticed."

"That's my story, too. It's probably pretty common. You don't feel the emptiness until you slow down and take stock, whether someone or something forces you to or whether you're a rare wise being who knows to do it yourself." He traced the line of the horizon on her frozen winterscape near Pewaukee Lake. "I'm not making that mistake again."

"What happened to make you quit your job? If it's okay to ask."

"Sure." He settled his hand at the back of his neck, and as closely involved as she was with what he was saying, she couldn't help observing him with sheer pleasure, the stubble speckling his cheeks and jaw, the vibrantly alive eyes, the well-developed muscles in his arms and chest—and how intimate his immediate acceptance of her personal question felt. "Let's see, I was sitting in a late-afternoon meeting, reviewing a case that wasn't going well, and I suddenly couldn't breathe, had pains from chest to shoulder and could barely move my right arm."

"Oh my God." She gripped the couch arm to keep from flinging herself at him in retroactive fear. "You had a heart attack? So young?"

"Nah, my heart's fine. I had an attack brought on by overwork, stress and anxiety. My body's way of saying, 'Hey, dope, I don't want to be here and neither do you, but since you're too stupid to figure it out I'm getting your attention the only way I know how.'"

"So you're okay."

"You worried about me?" He flashed her a sexy look that made her catch her breath. "Don't be. I've never been better."

"And you've turned back to woodworking."

"I'm in the middle of making a bedside table." He stood suddenly; she felt the loss of him beside her. "Do you have your camera here?"

"It's in a box on the way to Florida."

"Ooh, not good." He reached down, pulled her off the couch. "We'll have to buy you one. Or I'll lend you mine while you're here. Then we'll go all over the city for the next couple of days and feed your soul."

She shook her head bemusedly, heart speeding with excitement at the idea of holding a camera again, yes, but mostly at the idea of spending all that time with Sawyer, that he wanted to spend it with her. "You certainly take charge."

"Only when I'm sure I'm right." He backed toward the living room door, pulling her along, not that she resisted.

"C'mon, let's hit Sentry and get dinner supplies. What are you in the mood for?"

You. "Oh, I guess a big salad with—"

"Steak." He made a sound of derision. "Salad. Girly eater."

"Caveman."

He turned at the back door, stopping abruptly so she nearly ran into his chest. She rebounded, half wishing she hadn't been able to stop her own momentum. He caught her elbows, brought her up nearly against him, not quite. "Caveman, yes."

She pushed back, but not very hard. "You promised."

"Argh. The damn promise." He reluctantly moved to one side, gestured her through the doorway half-filled by his body. She'd have to scoot close by him, turned either toward or away. "After you."

Fine. She decided on turned-away and slid by, brushing against him lightly as she passed. She heard him draw in a quick breath and felt vindicated. Teach him to play with fire.

Except the way she was burning she wasn't sure Sawyer was the only one tempting fate. Other boyfriends had made her feel respected, desired, but this remarkable fascination Sawyer had with her, insubstantial as it might be, and the electric force of his personality were heady and hard to resist.

She had to remember that Melanie was the one who professed to love Sawyer, the one who'd be living with him for some time. She had to forget that Sawyer seemed indifferent to Melanie's flirtations, which had redoubled since that one odd phone call. Alana had to think of her sister first, how much Melanie deserved a stable relationship.

Alana rubbed at her arms uncomfortably. Something about her logic regarding Melanie's chances with Sawyer was starting to ring false, which made her feel slightly panicky and she wasn't sure why. She crossed to her car, her buoyant mood bogged down in confusion.

At the supermarket, she parked, still unsettled, and they walked up the slope of the lot toward Sentry. The humidity was climbing, which ruined a perfectly good summer afternoon as far as Alana was concerned. But given that she was about to move to Orlando, she better get used to it, the average temperature in Florida's July was in the nineties, with jungle-like humidity. Every single day. She was pretty sure she'd get used to it.

Inside the supermarket, carriage rolling along—Sawyer volunteered to push—they started in the produce aisle after he jokingly suggested they skip it for a direct trip to the meat counter.

"Mushrooms." He picked up a package of baby portobellos. "Can't have a steak without mushrooms."

"Cooked on the grill, brushed with olive oil and thyme, maybe a little balsamic vinegar."

"Oh, you are speaking my language, woman."

Alana laughed and moved on, her down mood blasted out of existence by his sense of fun. Even in a supermarket. She felt bright and energized, half expecting the produce to wilt at her brilliance.

"You want salad, so lettuce…"

"Organic. Here. Though I haven't figured out why they only package the good-for-the-environment lettuce in hard plastic." She picked up a tub.

"See, that's the advantage of the Man Diet—no vegetables to poison you or the planet."

"Hmph. From what I've read, the meat industry does more damage."

"*My* meat does no damage." He waggled his eyebrows and she rolled her eyes. She'd bet that wasn't true at all. Women probably jumped off buildings in droves when he left them.

The idea made her uneasy mood surface again. She pushed

it away, helped gather other salad ingredients—carrots, scallions, cucumbers. "You and Melanie should start a garden out back. You can still plant lettuce and beets at this time of year."

"*Beets?* You have got to be kidding me." He picked out some cherry tomatoes. "You like these?"

"Love them. What kind of food did you eat growing up?"

"Traditional for the most part. Dad insisted on main meat and side starch. When he was away on business, Mom would go wild and serve soup or omelets, or even better, breakfast for dinner, like waffles with bacon. She'd experiment with ethnic foods, Oriental, Middle Eastern. Then dad would come home and it was back to pot roast and potatoes. His idea of adventurous foreign eating was lasagna. Snap peas?"

"Another favorite." She put a handful into a plastic bag.

"What about you?"

"Gran was a great cook. Before that, with Mom, we ate take out, frozen dinners and anything that came out of a can. I was in charge of cooking pretty often, but my skills were limited. I remember trying to make sense of recipes in Mom's *Joy of Cooking* once in a while, but we hardly had any ingredients in the house in the first place, and it was too much effort."

"Wow." He clutched celery to his chest. "I love that image. Celery?"

"Absolutely. Love what image?"

He put the celery in the cart. "You trying to make a normal family life for yourself and Melanie. It's poignant, really. I had no idea your mom was so…"

"Absent?" Alana shrugged. "Mom was…*is* a very magnetic, charming and interesting person. With absolute zero impulse control."

"More like Melanie, then. Eggplant?"

"Never."

"I feel the same way." He grinned and put it back. "So you take after your father?"

"I wish I could tell you. Never met the man, and Mom refuses to talk about him. But I always fantasized that he was just like me."

"Hmm." He held up two bags of bakery rolls, one white, one wheat. Alana pointed to wheat and he tossed it into the cart. "We're batting nearly a thousand on taste compatibility. And I'm sorry about you missing out on having a father. If I'd known I could have sent you mine."

"You didn't want him?"

"I'm joking. Mostly. Dad can be a tough person to love, but we all do." He stopped in front of the deli counter and examined the offerings. "My childhood was a catered picnic in comparison to yours."

"There's no point in comparing. We had life easier than others, who had it easier than plenty. When Gran and Grandad realized how bad things were with Mom, they snapped us right up."

"And you've lived happily ever after."

"So far, yes." She pointed through the glass case. "Sliced turkey for lunches?"

"As long as we can have salami, too."

"Psht, a no-brainer." She ordered the amounts, along with sliced cheese. "Meunster okay?"

"Can't live a day without it." He gaped at an enormous summer sausage behind the glass case. "You know mine is—"

"Not *one* more word." She was quite sure she had never, ever had this much fun in a supermarket. Sawyer was so alive and so enjoying himself—getting groceries, for heaven's sake.

"Yes, ma'am." He picked up a loaf of bread, passed it around his waist a few times, shot for the carriage...and missed. Laughed, scooped it up and deposited it more sedately among the salad items. "Basketball was never my thing."

Alana laughed again, from sheer happiness. If Sam risked a similar move and missed, he would have sulked. He and she used to get into so many disagreements over brands, calories, nutrition, price, she finally laid down the law that one or the other of them would go food shopping—usually her—but not both.

Shopping with Sawyer was fun. Dangerously fun. If nothing else, Alana would try to put more of this type of fun into her daily life from now on. A lesson well learned. And a way to take part of Sawyer to Florida with her. Which she might as well admit she wanted to do, even knowing his image and her fascination would fade within a week or so after leaving.

At the meat counter, he casually piled five or six steaks in the cart to make her laugh. They settled on a thick ribeye big enough for three or four, two if you listened to Sawyer, then pushed the cart down the cookie aisle where they both reached for Nutter Butters at the same time.

"My favorite."

"Mine, too." He held on when she tried to pull them toward the cart, which left them close together holding the crinkly plastic package aloft.

Alana should move, but his eyes seemed to be holding her where she was. "Alana, you are denying fate. We passed the Nutter Butter test. We are clearly destined for each other."

She tried to laugh, but it didn't work. "Cookies is the ultimate sign?"

"Sure." He moved closer. "Cookies."

She wanted to kiss him practically more than she wanted to go on breathing. But she wouldn't, not until she had this all squared away with her sister.

"I think..." She swallowed, tried again. "I think we should go buy some wine."

"I think that I haven't had this much fun in way too long." He let go of the package, took a reluctant step back and she put the Nutter Butters in the carriage, feeling as if she were under water, her movements slow and not quite real.

They finished the shopping and made it through the check-out line, fighting amicably over the bill which they finally agreed to split. Back home, they grilled the mushrooms and steaks, made the salad, heated the rolls and ate in the back-yard, candles on the table ready to light when it got dark. Simple good food. Alana drank too much wine and put her hand over her glass when Sawyer opened another bottle. More and she'd lie awake in the middle of the night with a headache and the sweats.

The utterly Alana-sensible nature of that thought disgusted her, so she took her hand off and gestured him—what the hell, to go ahead.

"Tell me, Alana." He finished pouring her wine and filled his own glass. "What's wrong with the world and how can we fix it?"

"People need to be nicer to each other."

"Good plan." He lifted his glass. "Here's to being nicer."

"And more polite."

"Yes, please, thank you, ma'am."

"More accepting of each other."

"Without exception."

"More love. More—"

"Fabulous sex."

She nearly spit out her wine laughing. "I suppose that would help."

"I have another great way we can help change the world."

She was about to giggle when she saw his face, serious in the dimming light.

"Let's get some candles going and I'll tell you."

"Is this what you and Debbie were talking about that you said you'd tell me later?"

"Yup." He used a long, slender butane lighter on several

candles, which flickered in the still air and lit their immediate area with a warm yellow glow. "My dad has been asking me to head our foundation, which I resisted...until now."

He told her the story, the building Debbie wanted him to buy, the studio spaces available, some individual artist's stories, his excitement over improving Milwaukee's position as a city that encouraged the profitability of creative arts. While he spoke, she felt a sweet ache widening in her chest. This man had real depth and a real desire to live his beliefs.

"So I am thinking seriously of pursuing the opportunity."

"Sawyer, it sounds perfect for you."

"I think so, too." He took a sip of wine. "And...now, tell me how you got into building management instead of photography."

"That's what my Grandad did." She put her glass on the table, couldn't resist another Nutter Butter, even though they were definitely not meant to be served with red wine. "He managed the Milwaukee bank building downtown. I helped him through high school and college to earn money, then after graduation I was ready to leave home, so when a job came up in Chicago I grabbed it."

"You enjoy it?"

"Sure." She nodded slowly too many times. He waited, watching her expectantly, knowing there was more to the story than "sure." "It's good work. I'm organized, good at problem-solving, good with people. I learned a lot."

"But..."

"Like you, I guess I want something that is useful to the world, but also feeds my soul."

His turn to nod. He looked very smug and a little triumphant; she couldn't for the life of her figure out why. Plus they'd been talking nonstop all evening, but now silence fell between them. Crickets chirped, lightning bugs flashed yellow around the bases of trees and between bushes. An occasional car engine sounded in the distance. What was he thinking?

"Tell me something." His voiced had deepened, he was swirling the red liquid in his glass, watching her. There was no longer anything smug in his gaze. "Alana."

"Yes?" Her voice came out a little breathless. The way he was speaking, the way he was looking at her made the darkness seem to close in around them. "Tell you what?"

"Tell me what you would have liked to do that night we had together."

"What?" She instinctively sat up straighter and brought her knees together. "Where did that come from?"

"Have you been able to think of anything else? I haven't."

"Melanie wants you, Sawyer." She automatically reached for the issue with her sister as if it were a weapon.

"Melanie is out tonight with another man."

For a second she was startled, thinking of that phone call, then she realized. "Edgar? He's just a coworker."

"Not Edgar. Some guy with a weird name. That artist she was talking about, the guy from the Third Ward. She said something about being good and not calling him, but then he called her and she couldn't say no."

Alana tried to get her wine-soaked brain to concentrate. This made no sense. Why would Melanie do this when all she talked about was getting together with Sawyer? "But she's been flirting like mad with you."

"Nothing is going to happen there, Alana. Melanie doesn't really want it to and neither do I. Not with what's between you and me."

Alana kept her features calm while dark excitement rose. Deep down, she already knew nothing would happen between him and Melanie. It was a relief to admit it. And also mildly upsetting, which didn't make sense. With the Melanie issue out of the way...

Help.

"I promised not to touch you. I'm not going to touch you.

But—" he put his wine on the picnic table and she braced herself "—you can always touch me…or yourself."

Oh, no. This was crazy. She was on fire, at the same time clenching her thighs prudishly together. She'd never…not in front of a man.

"Listen to what I want to do to you, Alana. Everything I planned to do when we woke up together on Friday and never got to. I've been tortured by the thought of it ever since. I want you to be tortured, too."

He spoke in a low, mesmerizing voice of undressing her slowly, watching her breasts emerge, free and heavy, from the bra she imprisoned them in and exploring her nipples with his tongue.

Her breath hitched in a gasp. He whispered her name, put his hand to his fly in a silent question.

She nodded as if she were in a dream, watched him unzip his shorts, pull open fabric to release his erection, pull the outer skin down to the base so the shaft strained hard and long.

The sight nearly brought her to the edge; she began trembling uncontrollably from nervous excitement.

"Your turn." His eyes shone in the candlelight. A warm breeze caressed her and she shivered, though she wasn't at all cold.

Why not, Alana? There was no reason now other than her silly virginal reluctance, which the wine had loosened, and the strange dark fear burning in her chest.

She opened her legs slowly, shyly, moved the material of her loose shorts aside, then her panties. He made a sharp sound of agonized approval which spurred her fingers on to start a rhythm. She stared at the ground in embarrassment at first, then the arousal took hold and freed her to be bolder. Soon she could look up and watch his hand working…then make ⸺lf meet his eyes. The connection raised the excitement impossibly higher. She stopped trembling, let out a soft moan of pleasure.

He went on, detailing his slow slide inside her, the way she'd feel on his cock, the way he wanted her face to look while he pumped her.

Alana tipped her head back, braced one knee up against the arm of her chair, wanting him so badly she nearly gave in, crossed the few feet between them and straddled him. *What was stopping her?*

"Then I'd turn you over. Kneel behind you…"

Too late. She lifted her head, wanting to see him when she came. Her fingers worked harder. She focused on his thick erection, then as her orgasm hit, she looked up, met his eyes, let out a soft cry, and saw the rush of his own climax seconds later.

They both collapsed in their chairs, panting, sated, smiling in the private darkness of their evening together.

Alana took in a long, stuttering breath. How had this happened? Sawyer hadn't touched her with his hands, but somehow he'd managed to touch her heart. The thrilling rush they just shared, which she'd never trusted another man enough to do, seemed as intimate as if they'd made love for real, skin on skin, arms around each other, bodies joined. What made her turn around so completely to trust this man?

It wasn't only the wine.

Hours later, in bed alone, predictably, Alana couldn't sleep. She could damn the red wine, but it wasn't only that. She'd gone to bed late after sitting out on the lawn with Sawyer, talking for hours, until the candles burned down to stumps. Very late. Way too late to take a sleeping pill. So she turned and twisted and dozed and turned and twisted some more.

So restful.

Finally, after dawn started to break, she gave up and got up, put on a robe she'd borrowed from Melanie and went downstairs, started her coffee and sat at the counter, sexy memories of the previous evening still burning through her, feeling happy and guilty and confused and elated and just about everything else she could feel.

Halfway into her coffee, she heard steps coming downstairs and braced herself. Not Melanie, too heavy. Sawyer? So early? She hadn't spent the night with him. He hadn't asked and she wasn't going to get that involved, not when she was about to leave town. Why commit emotional suicide when she didn't have to?

The footsteps turned the corner. Alana gaped at the unfamiliar male silhouette. Who the hell was this guy?

He crossed the threshold into the kitchen. Young. Torn, sagging jeans. Bedroom eyes. Piercing in his nose. *Oh, Mel.* The "dreaded" phone call, the date last night—the artist guy, here in the flesh.

"Hey." The man raised a hand in greeting. "How 'ya doing?"

"Uh…good morning?"

"You must be Melanie's sister."

"Yes."

"I'm Sledge. Nice ta meetcha."

Sledge. Oh, God.

"Do you want some coffee…Sledge?" She could not call him that. She wanted him to leave. She wanted to go upstairs and haul Melanie out of bed by her feet and scream at her. Not to make more snap judgments, but "Sledge" had the look of all Mel's other bad-boy mistakes. What happened to the new leaf she was turning over? What happened to Sawyer being The One? Did that make this guy The Two? Were The Three and The Four coming over tonight?

Her sister's light footsteps sounded pattering down the stairs; she rounded the staircase, hand on the banister, swinging in a wide gleeful circle, stopped still when she saw Alana in the kitchen, then came forward. Cautiously.

"Hey, Alana." Melanie glanced nervously at Sledge. "You're up early. I thought you'd still be asleep."

"Hoped, you mean."

Sledge glanced even more nervously between the sisters. "Yeah, uh, I think I'm gonna hit the road, thanks. Nice to meet you, Alana. Mel, hey, c'mere."

Alana stared at the table to avoid having to watch the slurpy kissing she could hear all too clearly coming from the back door. The exchange of thanks for a fantastic night. Sledge's promise to call soon. Melanie's wistful response, "That'd be nice."

Then Sledge stepping through the door, the sound of it closing behind him. Melanie turned, arms crossed across her chest. "I know what you're thinking."

"Really?"

"You're thinking, 'How could I pass up someone like Saw-yer for a creep like Sledge?'"

"That's pretty much it."

"I know." She fell onto a stool opposite Alana and scrubbed at her hair in frustration. "I really wanted to fall in love with Sawyer. But he's just so, I don't know... Boring."

Alana was so flabbergasted, she couldn't even speak.

"He's so vanilla. I like spice, I like danger, I like—"

"Idiots."

"I know." Melanie slumped mournfully onto the counter. "But I don't know how to stop. I tried to want Sawyer, I really did. It's just not in me."

"Sledge was, though, apparently."

"Ha, ha. And speaking of into, if you ask me, Sawyer is way into *you*. So what hope did I have anyway?"

Alana shrugged. Even her hair was blushing.

Melanie looked at her curiously. "A bottle and a half of wine missing. You have fun last night?"

Now even her eyeballs were blushing.

Melanie grinned unexpectedly. "Honey, if you weren't

going to Florida, I'd say you and Sawyer were perfect for each other."

Alana tried to breathe calming breaths through a massive adrenaline rush. "Because I'm boring, too?"

"You know what I mean. He's a great guy. And even though I want to kill you most of the time, you're a great person, too." She groaned and bonked her head down again on the counter. "Me, I give up. I'm doomed to have a miserable, horrible love life."

"With Sledge?"

Melanie laughed bitterly. "He won't call again. I know his type."

Alana said nothing. She did, too, thanks to her sister.

"So." Melanie turned to send her a sly look. "Did anything go on last night?"

"Not…really."

"But something did?" Melanie actually looked hopeful.

"Sort of. I wasn't really going to do anything until I knew for sure whether the two of you were together, but he said you were out with—"

"It's okay, Alana." She hauled herself upright, reached for Alana's arm and squeezed. "Don't worry, seriously. It was pretty obvious nothing was going to happen between us. All I could do was force myself to flirt and he obviously wasn't responding at all, so the whole thing was kind of torturous."

Alana let out her relief on a long breath. "Okay."

"Hmm." Melanie got a distinctly calculating gleam in her eye. "So now that's all out on the table…"

"Ye-e-s?"

Melanie's grin turned wicked. "There's absolutely nothing stopping you from going for it before you leave."

Which pretty much summed up Alana's take on the situation, too.

Her sister was right, and it scared her to death.

10

"COME ON, Edgar."

"You are *not* getting me onto one of those things."

"Edgar." Melanie grabbed his elbow to stop him from walking away. They were standing in Juneau Park, on Lake Michigan, by the Juneau Park Paddleboat Company. Out on the calm waters of the tree-lined lagoon, bobbing next to the narrow wooden pier, were hydro-bikes, available to be rented, ten dollars for half an hour. Who could resist?

Apparently Edgar.

"C'mon, we have enough time before we have to go back to work."

"You told me you wanted to go *by* the lake for lunch today. Not *on* it."

"I know, but this would be much more fun. We can rent one of the tandem ones and do it together." They were both wearing shorts, thanks to the new casual clothes policy for summertime that their boss Mr. Maniscotto actually unbent far enough to allow. To Melanie's surprise, Edgar looked really good in his shorts; it was first time she'd seen him wearing them. She'd assumed he'd have pale stick legs, but that was, ahem, not the case at all. He looked solidly in shape. And now that she was looking, his shoulders were broader than she had noticed before, and were those pectoral muscles pushing against the material of his T-shirt? "Do you work out, Edgar?"

He glared at her. "Flattery will get you nowhere."

"Darn it." She laughed, more startled than amused. Never occurred to her to flatter him. She just wanted to know, because if you ignored his helmet hair and the fact that his shorts were rust-red brown and his shirt blue-and-orange-striped, he actually looked hot. Melanie would make sure to parade him by Jenny when they got back to the office in case she ever managed to ditch her horrible boyfriend and Edgar broke up with Emma. "Then do it for me."

"You won't stop whining until I give in, will you?"

"Nope." She smiled cheerfully and pulled him to the rental counter. "Give in to your fate."

He sighed heavily. "I'm doomed."

"Look at it this way. If it's wonderful, you can bring Emma and she'll think you're the greatest for suggesting something so fun. If it's horrible, you won't have risked pissing her off. I can be your test case."

"That is *such* girl logic."

"Hey, I'm a girl." She requested a tandem bike from the friendly man behind the counter and dug out her wallet.

Edgar nudged her with his shoulder. "I'll pay."

"No way. I'm forcing you. I'll do it." She whipped out her ten dollars before he got his and surrendered her driver's license for collateral, then handed Edgar his bright orange life vest, which he put on scowling good-naturedly.

The hydro-bikes were bicycle frames mounted on bright yellow pontoons with regular handlebars and metal mesh baskets in front. The pedals drove an underwater propeller. Melanie climbed on carefully and settled into her seat while Edgar followed. The entire contraption was surprisingly stable, and after a minute of pedaling, which took more effort than she expected, even Edgar began looking relaxed. They needed a few minutes to figure out how to keep their pedaling speed and direction coordinated, but once they did that, they could glide over the water, enjoy the beautiful leafy willows lining the lagoon and the clean, sharp skyline of Milwaukee beyond.

"I saw Sledge yesterday." Edgar threw that line out and lapsed into silence.

Dread started churning in Melanie's stomach, harder than the water churning from their pedaling. She didn't know what she had to feel so guilty about, but Alana's outrage and now the thought of Edgar's disapproval made her want to leap off the hydro-bike and swim to Michigan.

No, that wasn't fair. She felt the guilt herself, too. Here she'd said she was starting over, finished with the wrong kind of guys. She'd focused on Sawyer as the perfect example of a man who would treat her well. But everything about him felt warm and sweet and brotherly, while one glance at Sledge turned everything hot and salty and lover-like.

And yet. When Sledge left her kitchen yesterday morning, she felt only emptiness, sadness and relief. Emptiness because she'd betrayed herself; sadness because she knew she had no real chance at happiness with him, that he wouldn't appear again except possibly for more sex—which she didn't think was all that great, frankly; and relief because with him gone, she could try again to make her life better. Going off a diet once didn't mean throwing in the towel and giving yourself license to pig.

"So, um, what did Sledge have to say?"

"More than he should have." Edgar's words came out short and choppy, not like himself at all.

"Are you angry at me?"

"Of course not." He stopped pedaling and turned toward her, his deep blue eyes warm with concern. "Why would I be angry at *you?*"

Melanie shrugged and ducked her head. "Everyone else is."

"Everyone else being...Alana? Not Sawyer..."

"No, not Sawyer. But yes, Alana. And me." She stopped pedaling, too, since with only her working they'd started going in a circle. "I know what he is, I know he's bad for me. I did it anyway, and I don't even know why. It's like an addiction."

"No, Melly, I don't think that's it." His voice was so tender she was afraid to look at him.

Afraid? Of *Edgar?* She made herself turn. "So what is it? I inherited my mother's insanity?"

"Nah. I'd guess you've got some low self-esteem issues, feeling for whatever reason that you're not worthy of being treated well."

Melanie's chest tightened; she fought to keep her voice light. "Maybe."

"Or fear of commitment. Choosing men you know you won't hang around because deep down you're afraid one will."

"Oh." Her best cheerful voice wavered. His gentle words were scaring her to death. It was safer to think of herself as a screwup or of all men as jerks than to examine why her relationships invariably failed. Being this scared of mere words could mean Edgar had hit on a painful truth.

"Maybe next time really get to know the guy before you let him in the bedroom."

She shrugged, she hoped carelessly. "I was trying to do that with Sawyer."

"Sawyer isn't the right man for you."

"I guess not." She shaded her eyes against the sun. "Because apparently he's in love with my sister."

Edgar whistled softly. "Ouch. I'm sorry."

"It's okay." She shook back her hair, wishing the strange weight in her chest would go away. "Since I haven't been able to make myself want him, she might as well."

"You think she does?"

"Yeah." She pictured Sawyer's handsome face and found she was relieved not to have to match herself up with him anymore. Because he wasn't right? Or because she'd escaped a relationship that might actually work? Why did matters of the heart have to be so damn complicated? "In fact, I think something went on last night between them, which is so unlike Alana. To be all happy about matching him up with me, and then to go for him herself? That's more like something I would do."

"Don't sell yourself short. He might be good for her."

"I think he could be." Melanie started pedaling again and said a sad, fond goodbye in her heart to the fantasy of Sawyer. "You should've met her last boyfriend. I couldn't *stand* him. He didn't speak, he droned. And fussy, down to every last little detail. I never sensed any passion between them, or any sense of fun. He was like another of her duties. I have no idea why she stayed with him so long."

"Relationships can become habits."

She wanted to ask him if his with Emma had become that way, but didn't dare.

"She left him right after he proposed, giant relief." They glided farther on the calm water, Melanie turning over thoughts about the mystery of Alana and Sam until it hit her. "Oh my God, maybe *she* has a fear of commitment, too!"

"Maybe she does."

"Oh, that would be so much fun." She was so excited she nearly steered them into a passing pedal boat. "All this time I thought I was the only dysfunctional one."

"Melanie, you're not dysfunctional, you are human. You didn't have the healthiest upbringing or role model for relationships your first eight years. Give yourself a break."

"Thanks, Eddie." The warmth that went through Melanie's body wasn't only from the sun. Once again Edgar made her feel better about herself, sometimes more than she thought she deserved. She hoped she made him feel that way, too. Seemed like she was always the one needing him.

"Edgar, I really didn't mean to get you out here so I could dump on you."

"Fuhgettaboutit, Melly. I was the one who brought up Sludge."

"Sludge!" She giggled so hard her feet slipped off the pedals and it took her two tries to find them again. "That's perfect. Now tell me something about you so I don't feel like I've bored you to death."

"You haven't. And there's not much to tell. My brother is coming to visit."

She stared in astonishment. "You have a brother? How could I not know this?"

He shrugged. "I probably never mentioned him."

"You're not close?"

"Nah. He's nothing like me."

"What is he like?" She couldn't believe there was this whole aspect of Edgar's life she knew nothing about. What else was there about him she didn't know? Had she spent so much time focused on herself she never bothered to find out?

Ouch. The leaf she needed to turn over kept getting bigger.

"Let's see. Rock musician, heavy drinker, no college, no plans to settle, no financial sense, no discrimination where it comes to women. Shall I go on?"

"He sounds a mess." She tried not to think how he sounded exactly her type. No, her *old* type. "Why is he coming to visit? Where does he live?"

"Brooklyn. He's here for a gig at Shank Hall with his band, Imploding Bovines."

"Imploding... Never mind." She blew her bangs out of her eyes, getting winded, and embarrassed to admit it with Edgar next to her not even breathing hard. "What's his name?"

"Born Frank, now goes by Stoner." Edgar reached to turn her handlebars; the hydro-bike veered to face the sparkling expanse of the lake beyond their lagoon. "Look at that. Perfect day."

"It is." She allowed the abrupt change of subject, understanding that if he hadn't mentioned Stoner in the two years she'd known him, Edgar had a good reason for avoiding the subject of his brother. She wasn't often anxious to dish about Mom, either.

"I'm glad you made me do this, Mel. It's fun being out here with you."

"It's fun being anywhere with you, Eddie. You always make me feel so good." She stole a glance and found him staring out into the lake toward the invisible Michigan border. His plain face had never looked sweeter or more dear to her. "I know I've said this before, but I hope Emma knows how lucky she is."

"I'm lucky to have her, too." He met her eyes. His were so blue and sincere, hair blown away from his forehead, skin clear bronze, chin strong; he looked nearly handsome. "But I'm also really lucky to have you."

Melanie froze, half in delight, half in unexplainable fear. "Me?"

"Emma is the greatest, but she can't give me everything. Her needs are…simple, and mine are more complicated. It's really good to have you in my life, as well."

Melanie blinked away sudden tears and tried to smile. The sun was shining, breezes came softly off the lake. Her best buddy was paying tribute to their strong friendship. She had nothing to be crying over.

"If you leave yourself open, if you let yourself look with other than your eyes and your hormones, you will find someone worthy of you." His voice was low and sensual, very un-Edgar-like. "He may be closer than you think."

For one very odd moment, Melanie had the impression

that he was talking about himself. A certain look in his eyes, was it a trick of the sun? Edgar couldn't possibly…Emma was everything to him. But Melanie would swear he was hinting…

Oh, this was unbelievably awkward.

Edgar? She loved him but she could never. He was so…

He was so *sweet* and *thoughtful,* and supportive and caring and intelligent and funny and trustworthy, therefore someone she would never fall for in a million years, even if he was available.

It just freaking figured.

"Thank you, Edgar. I so appreciate your faith in me." She wanted to roll her eyes. *I so appreciate your faith in me?* Already he was pulling back, the light fading from his eyes.

"Should we go back?"

She nodded into the tension, trying to pretend everything was still normal between them, that she'd imagined what he was trying to say, that her reliable instinct had misfired big-time. She couldn't let anything hurt their friendship. She depended on him for so many things—laughter, great companionship, a sense of fun…

All the things she always said she wanted in a man. Sitting right there beside her in yet another surprise package she had no interest in opening.

11

ALANA WOKE UP with a sinking feeling that something was wrong. She stared at the ceiling, at the window. Beautiful sunny day again; what was the problem? Sawyer? Melanie? What was today? Tuesday. Hurricane day. She wished she'd gone with her instincts and traveled down to Florida. It was horrible being here unable to help, knowing Gran and Grandad were in danger and probably afraid. Hurricane Cynthia had made a slow, steady track directly for Orlando, in the center of the state, then suddenly veered north, staying a Category Two. But when Alana had spoken to Gran and Grandad the previous evening, it had already started raining, winds were up, there were reports of an extended storm surge at the coast, and it was still hours until the official landfall.

There was nothing worse than having to worry about loved ones in a situation she couldn't control. How often had she and Melanie lain in Alana's twin bed in their two-bedroom apartment in West Allis, wondering where their mother was, when she'd be coming back. Whether she was getting herself in trouble, drinking too much, being taken advantage of by some jerk. Whether that jerk would come home with her and live with them for a while, whether he'd be nice to them or bring creepy friends around who ate, smoke or snorted various substances and were generally terrifying.

A knock sounded at her door; Alana struggled up on her elbows. "Yes?"

"Are you decent?" Sawyer's deep voice.

"Sort of." Her blush was starting already, as was the adrenaline rush that leapt into action. He'd been gone a good part of yesterday—which gave Alana plenty of time to make minor repairs Melanie had neglected, and to clean more—but he'd come back to help haul stuff to Goodwill that Melanie had tossed into the basement rather than deal with. Alana had managed to avoid being in any intimate situations with him after dinner—and then was so tense and unsatisfied she'd had to take a sleeping pill in order to drop off.

Sometimes she felt like a mental case.

"Can I come in?"

"I don't— Yes, you can come in."

The door swung open. The white corner of a lap desk appeared, then arms carrying it, then a body. A fabulous body in jeans and a blue-and-white-striped shirt. On the lap table, a dish covered with an inverted bowl, a bud vase with a pink rose from the garden. "Breakfast is served, Madam."

"What—" She laughed in delight. "I've never had breakfast in bed. Unless I was sick."

"Then it's time you did." He whipped off the bowl covering the plate. "Scrambled eggs, toast with butter and honey, two strips of bacon, extra crispy, and a bowl of blueberries, raspberries and strawberries. Coffee is from Jamaica, with seconds available in the pot."

"I can't believe..." She gestured at the food. "Did Melanie help you?"

"Melanie is still asleep. But I quizzed her yesterday on your favorites. And here—" he produced the *Milwaukee Journal Sentinel* out from under his arm "—is your paper."

"Sawyer." She was oddly close to tears, even while she

couldn't stop grinning. So far she'd resisted the horrendous temptation to become involved with him, knowing she had to leave. But if he kept up this perfect-man stuff, she didn't know how long she could hold out. "I don't know what to say. This is all amazing."

"And so am I." He winked and backed toward the door. "Enjoy your breakfast."

"Thank you. So much." Alana only just managed to stop herself asking him not to go. Why would he want to stay here and watch her eat breakfast? She could deal with her worry all by herself—only now she'd get to worry on a full stomach with a fragrant and high-quality source of caffeine, brewed by a man she was afraid she'd fall for no matter what her common sense told her.

The eggs were delicious, creamy and rich, the toast crunchy and sweet, berries fruity and tart. She sighed blissfully at the last bite and unfolded the paper. An envelope fell out, *For Alana* written on the front in unfamiliar handwriting.

Inside, a single sheet of paper:

Your day belongs to me. Be at the Milwaukee Public Museum at 10:00 a.m. Enter through the parking garage. Sawyer

Oh, wow. She glanced impulsively at the clock. It was just past nine. But what did he mean, her day belonged to him?

"Alana?" Melanie this time.

"Yes, good morning." She hastily hid the note, not sure why she wanted to keep it from her sister.

"Hey." Melanie's blond head peeked around the door, eyes sparkling. "Isn't it time you dragged your butt out of bed and got going?"

"You know about this?"

"Oh, yes." She nodded somberly. "I was entrusted with

the important job of making sure you didn't stay home out of some misguided sense of duty."

"Misguided?" Alana shoved the tray away and got up onto her knees. "Gran and Grandad—"

"Will be fine. You know they will. And even if they're not, what can you do about it? Last I checked, weather was one of the few things out of your control."

"Oh, so funny." She scowled at her giggling sister and sat back on her heels. "Look, I can't go. I have to—"

"I figured you out, you know." She came into the room, arms crossed over her chest, looking smug as hell.

"Oh, really."

"You're scared."

"I'm—" She gaped. "Uh, what?"

"You're scared of what you feel for Sawyer," she repeated oh so patiently. "Scared that he's something really special. You want to stay and run away at the same time. You are drawn to being with him and also panicked at the thought."

"No, I'm—" Alana blinked. She was right about the feelings. But Alana wasn't going to admit it. "What makes you say that?"

"Ah." Melanie held up a finger, the brilliant lecturer getting to her most powerful point. "Because it's exactly what I do. I've figured this out, Alana, with Edgar's help. You and I exhibit opposite symptoms, but it's the same problem."

"Opposite symptoms…"

"I go out with wildly unsuitable men. You go out with boring unsuitable men."

She made a noise of outrage. "No, I—"

"You're telling me Sam was half as fun as Sawyer?"

"Well…" Oof. Not even half.

"Plus, take note, you dumped him the second he asked for commitment. And before him there was Alan, the economics major. Oh my God, I wanted to take a nap just from the way he said 'Hello.'"

"Alan was sweet."

"Yes, he was so-o-o swww…" She pretended to doze off, then jerked herself "awake." "He wasn't right for you. You're spirited and funny and indomitable. You need someone who matches you, not someone you can lead around by the nose."

Alana folded her arms defiantly. "I did *not* lead—"

"They all but whined 'Yes, dear' to everything you said."

More outrage noises. "No, they—"

"Alana." Melanie climbed onto the bed, knelt on her heels opposite, pulled Alana's arms uncrossed. "In every relationship you've ever had, who was in charge?"

"It was always fifty-fifty."

Melanie shook her head, eyes intent but not angry and thank God no longer smug. "Think about it. Just think. Major decisions, minor decisions, where you lived, where you ate, what you had in the refrigerator, how you spent your weekends…"

"No, Melanie, it was—"

"Don't answer yet." She took Alana's hands, gave them a little shake. "Just think. Honestly."

Alana made herself relax, closed her eyes, frowning, went back over memories, who decided what, how, when…

"Oh. Well… Maybe." She opened her eyes. "Yes, okay. I'm a dominatrix bitch."

"You haven't ever met a guy who really challenges you, who really is up to your level until Sawyer." She squeezed Alana's fingers. "It's exciting, isn't it."

Exciting? She felt absolutely miserable. Since when was Melanie the one giving romantic advice? Had Alana fallen this low without noticing?

"It takes you over, makes the world brighter, more exciting, like a drug rush without the bad health effects."

"Sort of." The words barely came out. Melanie's theory better turn out to be as ridiculous as it sounded.

"Welcome to my world. Except no, your world is ten times better. Because Sawyer is an incredible guy." She dropped Alana's hands. "A guy who could make you happier than anyone ever has. And if you ask me, you're already half in love with him anyway, so why not—"

"Wait, whoa, Melanie." She rose to kneeling in a ludicrous bid to be bigger than her sister. "I'm going to Florida, probably tomorrow, so what's the point?"

"You don't have to go."

Et tu, Melanie? She bounced off the bed, started pacing. "Of course I have to go. I have an apartment, a job, Gran and Grandad to take care of…"

Melanie shrugged. "Okay."

Alana stopped pacing. Not like her sister to give up that easily.

"Buk…buk…" Melanie started a weird jerking motion with her head, doubled her arms and flapped them like a chicken. "Buk…buk…buh-*keek*."

Alana giggled in spite of herself. "Cut that out."

"Just keep in mind what I said, okay?" Melanie waddled on her knees off the bed and clamped her hand on Alana's wrist. "I'll be home if they call. You get dressed and go to the museum. I'll call your cell if I hear anything. No, don't object, let me take some of the duty for a change. It will be good for me. Heck, maybe I'll even freak you out completely and clean up my room since you've done the rest of the house."

"Not the attic yet." Or the windows. She hoped it wouldn't come to that.

"God, Alana, you need serious help. Go. Git. Don't come back until Sawyer is done with you." She swatted Alana on the hip, then gathered her into a warm, impulsive hug. "And *promise* me. *Promise me* you'll think about how many people it's really your job to keep happy besides yourself."

ALANA PULLED INTO the public museum parking lot, nervous and jumpy. She assumed she and Sawyer were going to spend a sedate hour or two inside—what was so threatening about that?

Obviously Melanie's little talk had left Alana feeling off balance, vulnerable, uncertain. She hadn't felt this way in a long time. Once Gran and Grandad gave her life ballast, she'd thrived, applied herself to her studies, to her work with Grandad, to her dream of becoming a brilliant, famous and well-compensated photographer.

Yes, well, everyone needed dreams.

When her relationship with Alan went belly-up, she was on the verge of graduating and moving to Chicago; when her relationship with Sam ended, she'd eventually decided to move to Florida. Always a clear purpose. Always a clear idea of who she was and what she wanted and why.

Now…fear of commitment? Deliberately seeking out unsuitable men who wouldn't challenge her safe version of herself? She could laugh the whole thing off except Melanie's theories definitely struck some kind of chord.

Since when was Melanie the "together" sister? Since when was she the one stepping back to figure life out rather than drifting from moment to feel-good moment? Maybe she really was turning over a new leaf, Sledge notwithstanding. Maybe she really would evolve. Why did that make Alana feel stuck behind in her old rutty self?

She needed to shake off the uneasiness, have casual fun with Sawyer today and leave for Florida first thing in the morning, back on track. She hadn't watched her mother throw her life away on one man after another without having learned the importance of counting only on herself. She was strong, she was woman, she could enjoy this day without getting irretrievably deep into feelings for Sawyer, and have fun memories when she moved on with what she was meant to do. What she *wanted* to do. Someday she'd meet the right man at the right time who fit in with her plans.

Good.

She eased her Prius into a parking space, crossed the garage to the museum entrance, heels tapping sharply on the concrete, barely audible over the noise of the air circulation system. Once inside, she strode down the long corridor, past the colorful museum shop, toward the staircase to the exhibit space.

Would he meet her there? He hadn't arrived yet. She turned...and saw him behind her, halfway down the hallway, approaching in his loose, masculine gait, comfortable and at ease as usual. She grinned and felt herself relaxing. This would be fun. She could handle keeping things light between them and emerge unscathed to tell the tale, not out of Melanie's "fear of commitment," but just because it was the healthiest and most sensible way to handle her feelings.

"Hi there." He kissed her cheek, apparently having done away with his no-touching rule. She wouldn't object.

"Two surprises in one day, breakfast and now a museum expedition. What have I done to deserve this?"

"It's more what you don't deserve." He held out a green paper entrance bracelet for her to wrap around her wrist. How had he managed to buy tickets already? "You don't deserve to stay home cleaning on your last day."

The phrase *last day* twisted her stomach.

Steady.

"C'mon." He took her hand and they started up the stairs to the second floor.

"What are we seeing?"

"Butterflies. The live ones."

"I don't know that exhibit." She'd been through the museum countless times. "Wait, yes, I remember reading articles when it was built."

"You'll love it." He pulled her close as they mounted the

stairs and put his lips to her ear. "And by the way, you look incredibly sexy in those red shorts. Almost as sexy as you looked in bed when I brought you breakfast. It was all I could do to leave the room."

It was all Alana could do to laugh off his compliment when she wanted to say to hell with her resolve, drag him home, strip him and beg for sex.

Was this what Melanie felt? Was Sawyer Alana's "dangerous" man? Her Sledge? Maybe she needed to have a little more compassion for Melanie's…active social life.

"Hey, Alana."

"Mmm?"

"I know that face. You're overthinking." He shook his head sternly. "Today is about fun. Leave the cerebral stuff for tomorrow."

She smiled and collected herself again. He was just a man she'd met and enjoyed. Nothing about her life had changed. She was going to be fine. "It's a deal."

They got into line for the popular exhibit, then spent a few minutes with their designated group in a small transition area before they were admitted, to make sure no butterflies escaped.

The two-story glassed-in room was swarming with all types, colors and shapes, including, behind one special pane, various stages of caterpillar, chrysalis and emerging adults. In the open room around various flowering plants and trees adult insects fluttered free, landing on walls, greenery and awestruck visitors, who'd lowered their voices instinctively once inside, adding to the enchantment.

The creatures were so beautiful, so delicate, and right here, all around. Alana wished she had—

A cold metallic rectangle was put into her hand. She looked down, then up at Sawyer in amazement. "What's this?"

"Thought you'd want to take a few pictures."

She was beside herself. "How did you know?"

"Because you're a visual person with a lot of talent."

"Wow." She swallowed hard. "Wow. Thank you."

She turned away, ostensibly to find her first shot, but more to steady herself again. His understanding and belief in her was a precious gift that made her even more vulnerable than his attempts at seduction.

A swallowtail on the edge of a leaf caught her focus—hers and the camera's. She got the shot, repositioned for a better angle and took another, then another. She'd so missed having a camera as her second set of eyes. Why had she abandoned it? Catching fire, she started working the room, watching, observing, letting the pictures come to her. Two of the same orange species side by side on the edge of a planter, one with wings out, one with wings folded. The small yellow butterfly clinging to the letter T of the word *Death* on a teenager's jet-black T-shirt. The dark-eyed little girl barely containing her joy at being face-to-face with a monarch. Energy and effort-less concentration, marred only by her constant awareness of a certain man watching her enjoy the immense satisfaction of creation.

She was happy. Truly and deeply happy in this moment, doing what she was doing. With Sawyer.

Just call her Melanie For a Day.

He came up close behind her, where she stood hoping a blue butterfly would move ju-u-ust slightly to its right. He put his hand on the curve of her hip. She felt his size, the warmth of his body, the power of the Alana-magnets. This time she didn't resist, moved back pretending to need photographic perspective, pushing her rear gently into the fly of his jeans. Feel good in the moment. To hell with tomorrow. Sawyer and his camera had freed her to do that.

A low groan came out of him. "What are you doing to me?"

"Oh, sorry, was I doing something to you?" She clicked

her camera, even though she had no idea what she was shooting.

"Evil, evil woman." He pressed hard against her and released, tugging quickly on his jeans. "Here I was just trying to stimulate your...creativity."

"I don't think that's all you were— Look." She hardly dared move. A brilliant blue butterfly had landed on her forearm. She turned her head as slowly as she could, lifted the camera and tried to frame a decent shot, taking in the visible foliage, the fleshy bar of her arm juxtaposed against the brilliant blue wings, the spidery legs clinging to her skin, delicate fuzzy antennae, buggy eyes. The camera clicked, then again; the butterfly flew away.

Alana turned impulsively and kissed Sawyer on the cheek. "Thank you so much."

"For?" His arms came around her.

How could she explain adequately? "The camera. This trip. Everything. I didn't realize how much I missed taking pictures."

"You're welcome." His hand slid under her waist-length yellow top; his palm rested against the bare skin of her back. "Alana."

"Wait, don't move." A butterfly had landed in his thick hair, and was exploring the strands tentatively. "There's one on your head."

She stepped back, put the camera up to frame the shot. White butterfly on dark hair of gorgeous man, green branch dangling leaves close to them both. She got the shot, took another. Not surprisingly, he had a face the camera loved. Great planes, angles, good bones, and that look in his eye...

She lowered the camera slowly, allowing some of the warmth of his gaze into hers.

Yes.

Whatever he wanted, the answer was yes. It seemed like a silly waste of time to have avoided him for so long. Who was that uptight woman and what was her problem? To be desired and to be understood was everything a woman could want. Even a short time was better than never. "Were you going to ask me something?"

"If you were finished taking pictures?" He beckoned her toward him, put an arm around her, whispered in her ear. "Because you are desperately sexy when you work, and if I start kissing you now the way I want to, I'm afraid these little guys will be offended."

The butterfly in his hair bolted.

"See?" He didn't follow its fluttery path, kept his eyes fixed on Alana's. "Offended."

"Hmm." She pretended to consider. "Were you planning to start this kissing soon?"

"Oh, yes."

"Well, good," she said simply. She followed him to the exhibit exit, shaky and giddy-nervous. She'd been kissed plenty in her life. How did the promise of a few more manage to reduce her to gelatin?

Outside the enclosed exhibit, Sawyer strode ahead so fast she practically had to run to keep up. "Are we...going... home?"

"Nope." He ducked into a small-insect exhibit, made a sound of frustration when he saw a family there. "Wait, I know."

They went into the rain forest room, climbed the stairs into the virtual treetops and found...too many people.

"Okay. No. Here." He led her back down the steps and into a dark, abandoned corner. When his lips were half an inch from hers, her body already sparking, two teenagers came by and started examining photographs of cells, talking loudly in half-mature cracking voices.

Sawyer actually growled.

Another corner, this time a projection room where a few tired patrons could sit and watch a short movie. She followed him, pretty sure she'd come here on a school trip and watched it twice to rest her feet. "Hey, I remember this— Mmph."

Further thought fled with her physical ability to finish the sentence. She was being kissed. And how. Backed against the wall, a long denim leg inserted between hers. She welcomed it, wrapped her left leg around it and pushed rhythmically.

"Alana." He sounded hoarse, frustrated. She felt the same. "I want you so badly."

"Me, too."

"Today."

"Yes." She forced herself to think. "Melanie's home, but if we sneak in quietly, I've got clean sheets that we can—"

"Clean sheets?" He pulled back, looked at her incredulously. "I'm ready to go right here against the wall and you want to drive home and change your sheets?"

"I…well…" She made a silly face to hide how crestfallen she was. "I'm no fun, huh?"

He laughed, rested his forehead against hers. "I think maybe it's been too long since you let yourself have any."

She wasn't so sure she'd ever "let herself" do anything he was thinking of, but she wasn't going to admit that she'd been boring all her life.

Wait.

Not sensible? Not rational? *Boring?*

Really?

Dear God. This was turning out to be quite the day for destroying illusions about herself. Or maybe it was her turn to evolve.

"Come on." He kissed her quickly, then took her hand and led her out of the rainforest. "Change of plans."

"Please tell me you don't want to hump in the back of your car in the parking garage."

"Hey, there's a thought." He gave a fake enthusiastic thumbs-up. "Nah, I have more class than that."

"Whew."

He gazed at her with obvious affection, then lowered his head and kissed her again, differently this time, more the way he had that evening in the hallway outside her bathroom, gently, lingeringly, the way that left her a hollow shell of herself, a brainless, boneless mess of feelings.

One of which was fear.

Please don't let Melanie be right.

"Okay." He moved away reluctantly, smoothed back her hair. "We'll wait. Back on schedule."

She tried to shake away her odd mood. "Schedule? You do schedules?"

"I'm only Mr. Spontaneous in comparison to you."

She scowled in mock anger. "Evil, evil man."

"And to be honest. I have to be somewhere in about half an hour. Now that you've ruled out humping in the garage..."

"Ah." She tried desperately not to look disappointed.

He held out his hand. "But let's look around more while we can."

"Sounds good." No disappointment. Today was about fun, and she was going to have as much as she could, whether she was with Sawyer or not.

They walked through a few more exhibits, cowering playfully from the giant models of battling dinosaurs roaring thunderously through speakers, then picked out their favorite gemstones and minerals from the display case in the Earth section, and peeked into the windows of stores in the Streets of Old Wisconsin exhibit. Her good mood resurfaced from the sheer pleasure of being with him until he looked at his watch.

"I'm sorry, Alana."

"Time's up?"

He nodded regretfully. "For now. Let's go."

The parking garage seemed twice as unappealing on the way out as it had in, giant blowers roaring circulating air, low ceiling, concrete everywhere, all that was the same. But now she was leaving him, not going to meet him.

"Where's your car?"

Alana pointed listlessly; they wove their way through rows of vehicles in silence until they reached her Prius. Even humping in the backseat in semipublic was preferable to separating.

She had it bad.

"I had a great time." Sawyer kissed her sweetly. "We'll hook up sometime again later on today, okay?"

"Yes, sure." She started feeling that horrible vulnerability Melanie lived so often. Would he call? Was she being given a signal that all wasn't well in his feelings?

She turned firmly, opened her door and got into the car, hearing his footsteps hurrying away. This was ridiculous; she was not going to let this man turn her as crazy as her sister. No way. She slammed the door shut, shoved her key in, turned, and noticed an envelope under her windshield wiper. What the—

She glanced around, surprised when the envelope didn't appear to be on any other windshield. Was it the same type that had fallen out of her paper that morning?

She jumped out of the car, grabbed it and ripped it open. Inside was a piece of paper and what looked like a special key.

Feel like a romantic lunch at Coquette Café? I have a reservation at noon. Take this key and open locker B-7 in the museum before you go. See you there. Sawyer

Alana's cranky forehead smoothed; her lips relaxed, then curved into a smile; warmth bloomed through her.

Ohhhhh, wow.

She let herself fall back against the car like a lovesick fool, clutching the paper to her chest, grinning foolishly at the ugly concrete ceiling. He must have watched for her arrival and slipped the note on her car before he went into the museum to meet her.

He was *sooo* good.

Except—she glanced frantically at her watch—she'd need to rush home and change. Coquette Café wasn't stuffy, but it was fancy enough that she'd feel uncomfortable in casual shorts. Only, damn, she hadn't *brought* anything nice to Milwaukee. Hardly any of Melanie's tiny-boobed, thin-hipped funky stuff would fit her—literally or figuratively. As soon as she retrieved the treasure the key promised, she'd have to run by the Grand Avenue Mall on her way to the restaurant and pray she found something appropriate in ten minutes or less.

She locked the car and hurried back into the museum, got directions to the lockers at the information desk. A small alcove off the main entrance hall...found it...B-7...B-7...*there*. The key went in, turned. The door opened.

A shopping bag from Boston Store. She pulled it down, hardly daring to breathe, and looked inside. Tissue paper. And a note.

Melanie helped with this. She said you wouldn't be comfortable dressed casually at Coquette Café. She also said you wouldn't be caught dead in any of her clothes. Hope you like it. Sawyer

Alana pawed through the tissue paper, then gasped. He bought her a *dress?*

Yes. Royal blue with a subtle floral pattern, simple lines, scoop-neck, no sleeves. Not too fancy for the casual sandals she was wearing, but dressy enough for the restaurant.

Wow. In most cases she would not have been comfortable with a man she barely knew buying her clothes, but Sawyer—and Melanie—had saved her a mad dash through stores, or worse, feeling frumpy and self-conscious at the white-tablecloth bistro in shorts. She leaned against the lockers, dress held up to her shoulders, shaking her head helplessly. He was one in a million. Why did she have to meet him as soon as she was about to move away?

Because life was often like that—random, unfair, frustrating. She should have accepted that by now. There was plenty of bright side. Namely that the day wasn't even half over, a handsome escort waited for her at one of her favorite Milwaukee restaurants, and she'd rekindled her passion for photography, a joy that would last the rest of her life now that she understood better what it meant to her. So. No whining.

In the museum bathroom she stepped eagerly out of her shorts and threw off her top, pulled on the dress whose woven material felt soft and forgiving on her body. Hoping she wasn't guilty of pantylines, she exited the stall and tiptoed anxiously toward the mirror over the sink.

No worries. The neckline suited her; the jewel color flattered her skin even under horrid fluorescent lighting; her favorite silver twist earrings complemented the style; excitement brightened her eyes and flushed her cheeks.

She smiled at her reflection until a woman came into the bathroom with her young daughter, which made Alana bolt back to the stall, pack up her shorts and top in the shopping bag and his camera in her purse, and leave. Not a great idea to stand grinning foolishly at yourself in a public bathroom.

Out to her car in the parking garage which had reverted to being inoffensive, out into the sunshine of what had been and would now continue to be a blissful day, heading toward the Third Ward. On St. Paul Avenue, her cell rang. Melanie. Alana pulled over immediately opposite the Amtrak station and answered with shaking hands, guilty for not thinking about Gran and Grandad every second of the morning. "Did you hear from them?"

"They're fine! No worries. Cynthia is moving quickly, they're in the shelter, safe and sound. They haven't even lost power. Gran said people are incredibly organized and patient and there's a great feeling of community while they weather the storm. Grandad has a chess game going and Gran figures she'll finish another sweater today."

"Oh, thank God!" Alana's spirits lifted even higher. "That's wonderful."

"So don't worry and enjoy your date. Sawyer is a serious sweetheart. And a hottie." She snorted. "A sweet-hottie. I really can't believe I let *you* get him."

"He's a good guy." Alana laughed at the understatement. "Oh, and thanks for the dress, Mel."

"I wanted to get you something slit to there and tight, tight, tight, but he said no and picked that one out for you."

"Really?" Her glow intensified, mixing with happiness that her grandparents were safe. That was the main thing. And hey, if, when they got out of the shelter, they discovered their condo was ruined, maybe they'd come back home to Milwaukee and she could stay here with Sawyer and—

She said goodbye to her sister, hung up and drove on toward Milwaukee Street. No way could she wish that on them. They'd chosen their new life in Orlando, they loved it down there, and Alana would, too.

Lunch was perfect, from the chilled roasted tomato soup to the delicious lamb sandwich served with thin, crisp, perfectly salted French fries, to the excellent wine, service and mmm, yes, company. Sawyer's eyes had lighted up at the sight of her in the dress; they talked easily throughout the meal then lingered over cups of strong coffee to combat wine-induced sleepiness.

"Come on." He paid the bill and escorted her to the exit. "I want to show you something."

"Okay." She said a silent "yes" of satisfaction that he hadn't finished with her yet and trailed his shiny red Lancer up Lakeshore Drive to the tony suburb of Whitefish Bay.

On Summit Avenue he parked in front of an enormous brick

Tudor. She hurried from her Prius to meet him at the base of the driveway, feeling as if they were blissfully reuniting when they'd been apart for all of ten minutes. She could get used—she *was* getting used to this. If Gran and Grandad were all right, maybe she could put off leaving another day...

What for? To prolong the agony?

When Melanie was seven, she'd managed to cut her finger deeply with a paper cutter. Alana had been stuck nursing her because their mother passed out every time she got a look at the injury—though Mom had come through in other ways, cuddling Melanie and reading to her in bed with Alana snuggled up next to them both, wishing with all her heart that could be a nightly ritual, even knowing it wasn't possible.

But while Alana had been in charge of changing her sister's dressings, she'd told Melanie over and over: it hurts less if you pull bandages off quickly, get the pain over with in one quick second rather than drawing it out.

That was how she'd deal with Sawyer. Pull him off her and get the worst of the pain over with in one quick second.

"Welcome to my home." He put his arm around her and the two of them stood gazing at the impressive structure, shaded by a towering maple that seemed to embrace the house. "I was the only brother who wanted it when my parents moved out, so I inherited."

"Are all your brothers local?"

"Finn is, he's an investment banker, lives in Fox Point. Tom is a plastic surgeon in Chicago. Mark is VP of an engineering company, currently working in Germany."

"Pretty high-powered family."

"Dad wouldn't have it any other way." He smiled wryly. "My grandfather didn't cut Dad any rich-boy slack, and Dad refused to do it for us, either."

"You don't respect that?"

"I do. Deeply. But Dad took it a little too far. None of us were allowed even to consider a career that wasn't a guaranteed top earner. We all buckled. Finn was a talented musician, Mark loved cartooning. Tom...well, Tom is who he should be. And I became a lawyer."

Alana winced. "And nearly paid with your health."

"Yeah, but I'm fine now, and have emerged from the Cult of Dad." He moved her to the front door. "We all have some dysfunction in our past. Otherwise we wouldn't be human."

"True." She understood better than he knew. She could hear all the pain behind the brief summary of his life, feel the loneliness and frustration of thwarted hopes. She wanted to go back in time and fix it all for him, but no one got that chance. You took what the world dealt and played the hand as best you could going forward.

"Let's see if you get to meet the nephew horde." He opened the front door with his key, stuck his head in. "Maria?"

No answer.

"Hmm, guess what?" He pulled Alana in and shut the door behind her, took her hands. "We're alone."

"Oh?" She blinked innocently.

He locked her hands behind his back, put his on her waist. "In a house."

"Mmm?"

"With bedrooms." He moved his pelvis against hers. "That have beds in them."

"Ohhh." Her innocent act fled, replaced by hunger. *Don't think, live in the moment and* do.

He kissed her, once, twice; passion began to ignite...then they both heard it: the roar of the garage door going up. The sound of an engine, young voices shouting over it out open car windows.

"Oh, for—" Sawyer smacked his hand on the wall above Alana's head, looking at her in baleful exasperation, which made her giggle.

"This way." He took her by the hand and led her through

to the basement, closing and locking the door behind him. "We'll hide down here."

"From the barbarian invasion?"

"They're great kids, all of them." He turned her toward him, tall and broad in the low-ceilinged, dimly lit room. "But I'm not in a babysitting mood."

"Mmm, me, neither." She gazed up at him, grinning, until the emotion became unbearably strong and she had to look away, nervous and unsettled, as if they'd just met. "This must be your workshop. And that's the table you're making?"

"None other."

Alana walked over to examine it, disturbed by how rattled she was, but impressed by the woodworking. She'd done plenty of fix-it carpentry, but never tried making any furniture from scratch. The piece was solidly and skillfully built, spare but graceful with long tapered legs and a single drawer, classic Shaker style. "This is beautiful."

"Thanks." He ran his hands over the smooth, flawless wood, and she impulsively yanked his camera out of her purse and snapped a picture, then another when he looked up, startled, and a third when he smiled.

"You'll e-mail me these pictures in Florida?"

His smile faltered. "Yeah. Sure."

"I'll print them out and send you hard copies if you want."

"Okay." He was looking at her thoughtfully, as if he wanted to say something, tapping his fingers on top of the unfinished table.

"Yes?"

"What?" He roused himself and moved toward her, that prowling swagger that made her turn shaky with nerves and longing.

"You wanted something?"

He gave her a look that told her exactly what he wanted. "Yes, I definitely do."

"Me, too," she whispered. She was still unsettled, but her body was telling her to go ahead more strongly than her brain objected.

"You're sure?"

She put her hands to his chest. "What would you say if I changed my mind and said no?"

"Too late."

His lips were familiar by now, but no less exciting. The kisses turned fiery immediately; Alana arched into him, aware of his arousal, wishing they weren't in a basement among tools and planks of wood, but in her bedroom with clean sheets and candles and smooth jazz on the radio.

Did that make her boring? She didn't know. But when his tongue explored her mouth, thrusting in a way that turned her central heating up to high, she lost track of the thought and dragged his shirt up, explored his smooth muscled skin. They had to stop sometime, they couldn't make love here among all this dusty stuff and with kids upstairs, but she wasn't sure she knew when she'd get the strength to—

"Mo-o-om, Jake hit me with a truck."

Alana started, then closed her eyes again when his tongue lightly stroked her neck, and his lips followed. She tipped her head to give him access, moaning her pleasure. "I wish we were in my bedroom."

"No kids?"

"And a bed."

"Ah, yes, the clean sheets." He pulled her dress up to her waist. "I think we can manage here just fine."

"With...no bed?"

He stopped in the act of pulling her dress off. "You've never had sex out of bed?"

She froze in horror. Oh my God. *Why* had she said that? He'd think she was a complete unsexy, unadventurous idiot.

"I'm sorry." He pulled her dress back down, took her in his arms. "I didn't mean to shock you."

No, no, this was worse. Now he thought she was horrified at the idea instead of at her own inexperience. *Fix it, Alana.* She was leaving in the morning, she wanted to make up for the time she'd wasted and have him as many times as they could manage it, no matter where or how. If she fell for him, so be it.

"I'm not shocked. I just…"

"What?" He rocked her back and forth, his erection pressed against her.

"I must seem pretty…staid."

"I'd say you've probably had staid lovers."

"Maybe…" She was trying very hard not to panic. He had probably done women all over the city in all kinds of wild and spontaneous places and she'd completely killed the moment worrying about beds with clean sheets, for God's sake. She needed to work to recapture the feeling in the butterfly exhibit, where she'd truly managed to drop the control freak, let go and be in the moment.

"You don't remember our night together, Alana, but I do. Every second. Trust me, I was not bored. Never did I feel the need to nap. Not at all. Even on drugs."

She laughed and felt better. A little. No, a lot. She was going to fix this.

"If you're not comfortable here, we can—"

"I'm very comfortable." She pulled her dress off, stopped herself from folding it and hanging it carefully across a chair. In fact, she tossed it onto his half-finished nightstand, then unhooked her bra and did the dress on the night table one better, by tossing it carelessly onto the floor. She didn't even look to see where it landed.

Sawyer made a surprised and helplessly aroused sound that turned her on even more—and increased her confidence. "You sure you want this here, Alana?"

She smiled seductively, put her hands to the elastic of her

panties, eased them down, kicked them across the room. "Do I look sure?"

He sucked in a harsh breath, lunged forward and lifted her onto him. "You look incredible."

"Thank you." She wrapped her legs around him, somehow sounding cool and calm when she was wildly, breathlessly excited. She'd never done anything like this. It felt freeing and dangerous and safe all at once—which was the only type of danger she could handle.

Sawyer carried her effortlessly over to a worktable, which she promised herself she wouldn't inspect for cleanliness, but couldn't help one peek.

"Wait." He put her down, whipped off his shirt and spread it on the table, then lifted her onto the soft fabric, nudging her legs apart.

"Are you always this thoughtful?"

"I thought I was being practical. Get splinters in your butt our first time and you won't want me again."

She cracked up. "That is *such* a guy thing to say."

"Isn't it? So is this." He knelt between her legs, his breath warm, kissed her intimately, his tongue and lips wet and wonderful. "You have the most beautiful—"

"Mo-om. I can't find my Spore disk."

"Did you check your backpack?"

Sawyer leaned his head despairingly on her thigh. "If it's not drugs or too-public places, it's children."

"We'll get it right." She stroked his hair affectionately, lingering on the curl around his ear, the thick strands at the bottom of his neck. She loved that when things went wrong he laughed and rolled with the punches. She could learn from him.

"All we have is today." He gazed up at her; the emotion smoldered, sparked, then burned clear, bright and steady until she had to look away again.

If this wasn't love, she had no idea what it could possibly be. She'd never felt anything like this before.

One day. Only one day to explore it.

He stood, moving his hands leisurely along her thighs, kissed her with increasing passion. She unsnapped, unzipped his jeans and pushed them down; he caught them with one hand behind his back and extracted a condom from the pocket.

"Ah, took me for granted?" Her fingers entered the fly of his boxers, catching his hard length in her fist.

Breath hissed between his teeth. "A man can always hope."

She leaned into his broad chest, played with his nipple, teeth and tongue causing soft moans that pleased her as much if not more than her touch pleased him. She loved the power she had to make him this aroused; the power he had to affect her so deeply. Her hands kept stroking his erection, exploring the juxtaposition of baby-soft skin and jutting hardness, until her need to feel him inside her began to be desperate. She shoved the material of his boxers down and away, setting him free. He was so beautiful, generous and smooth, sleek and eager.

"Now," she whispered. "While we can."

He rolled on the condom, then knelt and used his mouth to lubricate her. She arched her back, hands landing hard on the table behind her, while his tongue thrust inside her, painted the outside of her opening with moisture. Her breath accelerated; her heartbeat followed. Oh, what she'd missed that first night together by being asleep.

"Sawyer." She stopped for a whimper of pleasure. "I'm ready. Please."

She couldn't wait, wanted him inside her before they were interrupted, before she stopped to think how much more she'd love him after they were joined this way…and before she got so turned on she started screaming her frustration.

"Yes." He stood between her legs, wide shoulders, slender hips, solid and so male. One hand steadied her waist, the other guided the head of his penis. He paused as his breath released, then started a slow, strong slide inside her, setting nerve endings on fire.

What she thought would be most distasteful about having sex in a basement turned out to be the most arousing. She loved the hard, unforgiving surface under her, the occasional ache in her tailbone, the creak of the table, the wood and stain smells mingling with the heat they generated together. The sex felt rawer, more powerful, more urgent and animal, which turned her on out of her mind.

Or maybe it was just this man.

She brought her knees up high, loving the depth he could get in that position, loving even the flashes of pain when he moved deeper. She cried out, cried out again. His hand landed on her mouth, his thrusts increased speed. Alana blew out breath, felt the resulting dampness on the palm firmly denying her volume. The suppression, the mildest most innocent version of bondage possible turned her on even more. She grabbed his hips, urged him on. Just when she thought she'd explode with the desire to climax, his finger found her clitoris and within seconds the orgasm rocked her, filling her body with starburst sensations.

Instead of coming down, she was hit with a frenzy of fresh desire. He slowed to give her space to recover, but she shook her head, mumbled, "Keep going," behind his fingers.

He took his hand away. "Am I hurting you?"

"No," she panted. "Keep going. Keep going. Don't stop."

He groaned and increased his pace. She loved every sweaty, lustful minute.

Leaning back, she caressed her breast in a seductive circle with an open palm, watched his face responding, tightening, going blank as he withdrew into his own climax, then coming alive again as the peak tore through him.

Then his eyes met hers, he was breathing hard, face alight. She returned the smile tremulously, feeling dangerously vulnerable. All the more because of the new, deep emotions giving those feelings a solid foundation.

Please tell her he felt it, too…

"You okay?"

"More than."

"Did you miss a bed?"

"I will never use one again."

He chuckled. "They have their place. Come here."

She put her suddenly shaky legs back down, wrapped her arms around him, laid her head on his warm chest, inhaling his scent, trying to capture the moment, a mental snapshot she could keep forever. He held her tightly, stroked her hair, kissed it gently. "Don't move to Florida, Alana. Stay in Milwaukee with me."

Alana stopped breathing. Panic erased her bliss. "My grandparents need me. Gran fell stepping off a curb or something. She could have broken her hip. I would never forgive myself if something happened to either of them and I wasn't there to help."

She stopped the second she realized she was babbling idiotically. What was with that?

"I know. I understand." Sawyer kissed her, drew his thumb from the corner of her mouth across her cheek. "I'd beg for one more day together, but I have a feeling we could be together a hundred more days and it still wouldn't be enough."

Alana hid her face, nodding mutely in agreement, trying hard to calm herself, and trying harder not to hear Melanie shouting her told-you-so.

12

CANDLES. SAWYER FOUND the cabinet he'd opened his first official morning here, when he'd shared Raisin Bran with Alana, and pulled out a box of candles, hoping Mel and Alana would excuse his thievery—no time to buy any. He added the candles to the insulated bag he'd prepared while he was cooking Alana's breakfast, packed with dinner he'd take to his family's summer house on Lake Wishkitba, where he planned to spend what could be his last night with Alana. It didn't seem possible he could feel this deeply about someone and, having just found her, be preparing to say goodbye.

A glance at his watch told him he'd better hurry back to Milwaukee's lakefront to meet her for picture-taking. Half an hour ago he'd left her in the basement, pretending to need the bathroom, but had made her promise she'd check out the new drawer of his bedside table, as if he were wildly proud of it and needed admiration.

Inside the nearly finished drawer had been the last invitation. To meet him at Bradford Beach, where she'd taken that one incredible winter dawn picture. He wanted to give her the chance to recreate the picture, to have another memory of the city to torment her in Florida. Then he'd get her to the lake house for dinner and in-bed sex with candles the way she wanted, the way circumstances had prevented them from having yet. Alone. Uninterrupted.

He zipped the cooler closed. If anyone had told him even a week ago that he'd be planning to decorate a room to make it sweet and romantic for sex, he would have given whoever it was a manly sock in the jaw.

Alana had him. Any idea that she wasn't his "type" had been firmly subjugated to the intensity of his feelings. Never before had he felt this…*much*.

After the candlelit sex he wanted to hold her all night, and when it was time for her to leave the next morning, not let her go.

He couldn't keep her here. She felt she had a duty to her grandparents, which he understood and admired, even though he'd spent so long struggling to where he could finally understand that he also had a duty to himself. And he also suspected she was gun-shy about getting too involved too quickly, which, given her mother's apparent behavior, he also understood. If that were the only thing keeping her from staying, he'd do whatever he could, playing fair or foul to change her mind.

But…

He would love the chance to convince her to stay. Another day. Another week. Even if, by then, he'd be so crazy about her it would hurt ten times more when she left.

The house phone rang. He hesitated. Calls for him would come to his cell. But Melanie wasn't home, and the helpless grandparents could be calling again. He strode over to the wall phone, checked caller ID. Yes. Edwin P. Hawthorne, aka Grandad.

"Hello?"

"Oh…. Who is this?" The voice was surprisingly firm and cheerful. For some reason he expected Alana's grandmother to sound at death's door.

"Sawyer Kern." He wasn't sure he should identify himself

as Melanie's roommate in case she hadn't told them a man was living with her.

"Of course, Sawyer dear, it's nice to talk to you finally, Melanie's been keeping you from me. This is her grandmother, Edith Hawthorne."

"Nice to talk to you, too, Mrs. Hawthorne."

"No, no. Just Edith." She sounded younger than he expected, too.

"Edith. Is Cynthia gone yet?"

"Oh, yes. Just passed." She sounded completely matter-of-fact.

"Must have been frightening staying through it."

"I don't know, I found it quite exciting. Nature's power is truly awesome." A deep voice rumbled in the background, Edith's voice murmured a response. "Yes, tell the girls we've heard from the president of the association and our condo survived just fine. They shouldn't worry, though I'm sure Alana has anyway."

He chuckled. "Maybe a little."

"Poor thing. She gets so worked up. Always has. How are the girls getting along?"

"Uh." He had no idea how to tackle that one. "Okay."

"Not good, huh. I'd hoped by now… Well, it may take a few more years, but they'll end up best friends, you watch. They're more similar than they realize."

Interesting. He wanted to ask more, but wasn't sure it was his place. "Alana's looking forward to seeing you."

"Ah. Yes." She sounded distracted. "When is she coming now?"

"She's planning to leave in the morning."

"I see." She passed along that information in a loud whisper. The rumbling in the background responded again. "Thanks for letting us know."

Enthusiasm was missing from her tone. Sawyer's hope perked up its eternal ears. "That's not convenient?"

"Oh. It's fine. We'll adjust. She is so anxious to move down here…"

Sawyer walked to the window. "But?"

"Nothing, really. Edwin and I are a bit concerned about the timing."

"Because of your injury?"

"My what?" She sounded so astounded he started questioning whether he was mixing this story up with someone else's. Except Alana had mentioned it barely an hour ago.

"The leg you injured after your fall."

"Oh, that." She laughed dismissively. "I put a Band-Aid on the scrape, had bruises for a few days, that was it. I was back in my skates within a week."

"Your…skates?"

A louder rumble in the background. Edith gasped. "Oh, I wasn't supposed to tell. Rollerblades. Edwin and I have taken it up. We're having a ball down here."

Sawyer took two beats to be absolutely flabbergasted, then started grinning. "Do Alana and Melanie know how you hurt yourself?"

She cleared her throat uncomfortably; he grinned harder. "We…didn't want them worrying, imagining accidents and so on. We wear helmets and all the padding. All the folks do down here. It's very safe. I only fell because someone bumped into me while I was bent over fastening my skates. I'll do that in a chair from now on."

"Good idea." He rubbed his forehead, pacing the room now, not sure how much was appropriate to ask, but his immediate future—and maybe his heart—depended on her answer, and he wanted that answer spelled out in plain English before he'd trust it to be true. "So…you aren't relying on Alana to take care of you?"

She sighed. "Alana needs to be needed. Her mother, our daughter…well, maybe they've told you."

"Some, yes." He still didn't have what he wanted, but that

was close enough to make him want to leap around like a complete fool. Alana wanted someone to need her? He was all over that. "You mentioned the timing of her visit being off."

"Oh, yes. See, after the hurricane settles down, we're planning to drive to Lake Wales to try our first time skydiving. But if she's arriving soon, we'll postpone it."

"That would be a shame." Shame—something he was completely without at the moment. "Can't you go after she gets there?"

"Well, to be honest..." She laughed uneasily. "I'm not sure she'd let us. We've always wanted to do this. I suppose it's on our bucket list, like it was on Jack Nicholson and Morgan Freeman's in that movie, except we're not ill, just not getting younger. After we moved down here, we were talking one day and said why not do it? You can talk things to death, but sometimes you have to get up and act."

"I agree." Skydiving! He was nearly as crazy about Alana's grandmother as he was about Alana. "So if I'm getting this right, you're afraid Alana moving to Florida will cramp your style."

"Oh, no, no *no,* of course we're dying to see her, we adore her and Melanie both, and it will be wonderful having Alana close by..."

"But?" Shameless. He'd even stopped feeling guilty for pushing her. At this point, he was a shark who'd smelled prey and would circle relentlessly until he got what he was after.

"Well, to be honest, we've gotten used to being independent. We're finally having that delayed empty nest, you know, and...well, I feel terrible telling you all this. Edwin is sitting here shaking his head, scowling at me for rambling on. But then you're practically part of the family."

He hoped to be. Maybe. Someday. If everything worked out with Alana the way he felt it should. "I completely understand. I won't say a word to either of your granddaughters about the skydiving. That's yours to tell. But I might be able to help you keep the nest empty, at least for a while longer."

"Oh? Yes? What do you think we should do? Talk to her, I suppose."

Sawyer laughed. His mood had turned around one hundred and eighty degrees. The gloves were off. He'd do whatever it took to keep Alana here in Milwaukee where she belonged. "Tell you what, Edith. Why don't you and your husband leave all that up to me?"

"You DITCHED ME again."

Sawyer grinned. She was gorgeous, standing patiently waiting for him at the fairly crowded beach house. Even more gorgeous than she'd been so recently when he 'ditched her again' in his basement. She'd changed back into the red shorts that exposed her shapely legs—strong thighs, round calves, trim ankles—and the soft yellow top, which hugged her hourglass figure and made it difficult to remember he owed her a response.

"Hey, you know, I'm a love-'em-and-leave-'em kind of guy."

"That right?" The tiniest anxiety in her voice.

"Actually, no." He bent and kissed her soft mouth. "Leaving's your job."

"I know." Her features saddened. He tried not to smirk. Alana didn't know it yet, but she wasn't leaving. Tonight's mission was to get her promise to stay another day or two…or three. Buy him time to visit the foundation and put his hat in the ring for the director's job—a formality, given his father's influence and desire he take the position—and work out the rest of the details for supporting Debbie's artist-studio building, see if she and her partners would agree to hire Alana to manage the building. A form of nepotism maybe, but she was well-qualified, having not only management experience but the artistic bent, as well. Until the property was renovated, she could work with him at the foundation. Or relax and let him be her sugar daddy for a while, not that he thought she'd agree to that arrangement.

He was getting way ahead of himself, daydreaming of a future together. Nothing he'd ever done before with other girlfriends, especially not within days of their first meeting.

"I spoke to your grandmother."

Her eyes lit—cautiously. "She's okay?"

"More than okay. They've heard there was no damage to their condo. I left Melanie a note."

Alana frowned. "She wasn't home? She promised to stay home just in case."

"Hey." He kept his voice gentle. "You told me at lunch they were okay, remember? She probably thought it was safe to leave the house once Cynthia passed."

"Okay. You're right." She closed her eyes, shaking her head. "I'm worrying too much. Again."

"Don't need to this time, I promise." He pointed up the beach. "Want to take a walk?"

She nodded and fell into step with him. Sawyer opened his mouth and geared himself up for a big fat lie—he hoped the only one he'd ever tell her. "They also said the roads are bad. Trees down everywhere, debris on the highways. They told you not to come yet. It's still dangerous. Give the cleanup crews a few days to get things done first."

"A few days?" She frowned. "But I want to make sure—"

"They're fine, Alana, I promise. Your grandmother sounded cheerful and happy, as if she enjoyed the whole thing." He turned, brushed hair off her forehead the breeze was threatening to push into her eyes. "It's me that really needs you."

"Oh?" She tried to look suspicious, but a smile pushed at her lips. "What do *you* need me for?"

He held up fingers to count. "Cooking, cleaning, mending, picking up my dry cleaning, giving me on-demand blow—"

"I don't *think* so, caveman." She suppressed a giggle and took off walking.

"Okay. Not that." He caught up to her and grabbed her hand, swung it gently between them. "But if you ask me, what's between us is pretty special, Alana. Maybe you don't agree…"

Her pause, all of two seconds long, seemed to go on forever. "I do."

"So?" He had to tamp down his adrenaline or he really would start with the leaping for joy. "If they're okay without you and I'm not…"

She pursed her lips, but at least didn't reject him outright. "Did Gran say anything about her leg?"

"I mentioned it, and she acted as if the injury were so minor I was weird for asking."

"That's Gran. A total stoic."

Hmm. He'd have to pound that one home a little harder. "She said she's back doing, um, everything she was doing before."

"It could happen again." Alana bit her lip. "Did she say what caused the fall?"

"She was bending over fastening her…footwear, when someone bumped into her. She promised to do all her footwear-fastening seated from now on."

"Oh, gosh, so her balance isn't what it was. I'm really wor—"

"Alana." He stopped walking. This had gone far enough.

"What?"

"Bend over."

"What?"

He pretended innocence. "What, you haven't had doggie sex in public in broad daylight before?"

She burst out laughing. "Geez. Listen to you."

"Seriously, don't knock it 'til you've—"

"Sawyer."

He relented. "Pretend you're tying your shoe. I promise I have a point."

She rolled her eyes and bent over. It was all he could do not to grab on and experience heaven, but it *was* public and daylight and he *did* have a point. It took only a gentle push followed by a quick grab to keep her toppling onto the sand.

"Wow, your balance isn't what it was, Alana. I'm really worried."

She stood and glared at him, color high in her cheeks, eyes dancing. "Fine. You won."

"Not until you say you'll stay. Then I win."

She exhaled, made a helpless gesture with her arms. He caught her in his arms and kissed her forehead, her cheeks. "Come on. Let me win."

She pretended exasperation, but her full, sexy lips were trying very hard not to smile. "Okay. If they don't need me yet. A few days only."

"Thank you." He let out a breath, pointed to a seagull perched on a beach towel, and when she turned to look, allowed himself a silent, high-fisted *yes-s-s* behind her back before he started them walking again to the north, where the beach curved and the best view of the city would rise behind them. "You have my camera?"

"Of course." She dug it out of her bag. "Hold still."

He put a hand in front of his face. "Not me, a picture of the city."

"I will. But I'll want pictures of you, too."

"You'll forget me otherwise?"

She gave him a sassy grin over the camera. "In a heartbeat."

"What if you had me every day to look at? In the flesh." He stood for another picture, hands on his hips, wondering how far she'd go, if she felt as deeply as he did, loathing his vulnerability as strongly as he was determined to keep her here.

She took a step back, focused her lens. "What, you're going to move to Florida, too?"

"No. You're going to stay here." He smiled. The camera clicked.

"You think so?"

"Milwaukee is your home. Florida is torturously hot eight months of the year. Milwaukee is only torturously cold for four."

"Where did you make up those statistics?" She circled around him, taking more pictures.

"I saw them online."

"Yeah? What site?"

"Madeupstuff.com."

"Ah." She clicked the lens again, walking backward while he advanced on her.

"*And* Florida has cockroaches the size of New Jersey."

"Those are palmetto bugs."

"They're cockroaches. Friends of mine who lived in Orlando had slimy slug trails on their living room walls every morning, frogs hopping around the house, crickets, lizards. When they moved, there was a menagerie of death under the piano where the cat had chased them all."

She stopped taking pictures. "Ew, really?"

"I swear." He made an *X* over his heart. She clicked the camera. "And there's no bratwurst, no custard…"

"No shoveling, no icy roads."

"Black ice. They have that. And horrible traffic."

"Year-round barbecues."

"No me. No us." He lunged forward, stopped her walking away from him. "Only Milwaukee has us."

She kissed him as eagerly as he kissed her. The part of his brain that could still think remembered what her grandmother had said about her and Melanie being more alike than they thought. Beneath Melanie's passion there must be a practical streak, because certainly beneath Alana's practical streak there was passion. And how. He wanted to unearth all of it, push her to the border of what she could handle, sexually and emotionally. He couldn't bear the thought of any Florida guy making those incredible discoveries.

"Let's take a picture of both of us." She dropped to her knees, beckoning him to join her, put her bag on the sand and adjusted the camera until she could get the shot she wanted. She set the timer, hurried next to him, and slid her arm around him the same time he slid his around her and hauled her close, mugging for the camera even as his body registered how good hers felt next to him.

She fit him. Better than his friends, his family, better than himself. She brought out the fun in everyday doings that he had lost track of, that he'd spent the past months trying too hard with too little success to capture after he quit his former life. Most valuably, she'd inspired him to look to his future with something other than pressured disinterest.

Alana was good for him. Other women had been nice companions, pleasant lovers, but he never felt any of them belonged in his life the way he felt Alana did.

"One more." She reset the timer, posed again, then broke her radiant for-the-camera smile with all-out laughter when he tickled her. "Hey!"

She brought up the picture in the viewer, studied it and handed the camera to him, her smile turned more serious. He looked. Shook his head, handed the camera back. "You ever see two happier people?"

Alana looked again, biting her lip. "No."

"You won't know anyone down there."

"I'll make friends."

He shrugged, pretended to let it drop. He'd gotten her to stay another few days or so, and had planted the seed of forever. He gestured to the lake, to the greenery lining the shore, to the city skyline a mile to the south. "Take more pictures.

So when you move to Florida you can take Milwaukee with you."

"I'd like that." She stood for a moment facing the city, the sun heading toward the west for its eventual night's rest glowing on her face, lighting her eyes, which were slightly troubled.

It was all he could do to keep himself from saying it, and in the next second he forgot why he shouldn't and gave in, throwing common sense and pride to the Lake Michigan winds.

"Alana, I love you."

13

SAWYER'S SUMMER PLACE was beautiful, nestled among firs, oaks, maples and birches at the edge of the small lake, which, with the surrounding land, belonged entirely to the Dalton/Kern family. The house was a cozy little six-bedroom—just the thing for a casual weekend away from their other cozy six-bedroom on Lake Michigan.

So maybe she was a little awed and a little bitter. It was hard to imagine having this much room to move around in without inflicting yourself on anyone else. Not another house in sight; the lake, vaguely kidney-shaped, might as well have been in the wilds of Alaska.

Which for this evening suited Alana just fine. How long she'd stay in Milwaukee before making the trip to Florida she didn't know, but a huge weight had lifted when Sawyer convinced her to stay these few extra days…not that he'd had to work too hard to change her mind.

How long since she'd taken a vacation? Too long. She'd worked with Grandad year-round, through summers, through college, then taken the week between graduation and starting her job in Chicago to move and get settled.

"I'll show you around." Sawyer grabbed the cooler from

the trunk where it had thudded back and forth during their hour's drive from Milwaukee.

"I'd love that." She got out of the car and inhaled the warm woodsy air, slapped at the mosquito trying to welcome her to Lake Wishkitba.

What would have happened if she'd decided not to come to Milwaukee, to leave Melanie to her own mess this time? She'd be in Orlando now, having just been through a hurricane. The outgoing manager of Shady Oaks Condos would have to cope with the cleanup, but she'd probably have been called in to help even though she didn't start officially for another week. Instead, she was here, toward the end of a perfect day, in a lakeside paradise with a man who said he loved her.

Loved her! When he'd said the miraculous phrase on Bradford Beach, she'd been paralyzed, torn between joy and shock so that she'd probably looked like a parody of a stunned person. Sawyer had laughed when he took her in his arms, told her not to say anything, that he'd been feeling it and wanted her to know. Again, the unflappable Sawyer, taking life as it came, though she could sense his disappointment. What would she give for that easy nature? If she'd been in his place and gotten no response, she probably would have hurled herself face-first into the sand and howled.

She'd wanted to give him some indication that her feelings had progressed way beyond the initial thrill, too, but it was beyond her to make that kind of declaration. Not now. Maybe not ever. Even if this was the beginning of love—which was certainly possible, given that she'd never felt this way about anyone—it was love already doomed. In a few days she'd be starting an entirely new life. She didn't want to do that with half her heart bound to someone she'd left behind. Long-distance relationships satisfied no one.

A breeze came across the lake, bringing more forest fragrances. A chickadee hopped on a nearby branch, head tipped to watch them curiously. A squirrel scolded Sawyer for intruding on its territory; apparently it wasn't intimidated by the Dalton/Kern dynasty.

"Let's go in." Sawyer slapped a mosquito away from his ear. "Screened-in porch is a savior this time of year."

The house, shaded by trees, was decently cool. Unused in a while, it smelled of pine and a faint fragrance of cleaners and moth balls. The furniture was summery in florals and pastels, walls decorated with landscapes and occasional kid art, the kitchen any cook's dream, the dining room informal chic.

She helped Sawyer open windows. Then he disappeared upstairs to start the attic fan, which drew air inside and up through the house, soon replacing the unpleasant stuffiness with fresh grassy aromas.

"I brought you a change of clothes and toothbrush." He came back down, caught her examining a beautiful watercolor of the lake by a "Mark" she assumed was his brother. "I hope it was okay to go into your room back home and dig."

"Of course. You think of everything."

"I try." He put his arms to her shoulders, kissed her forehead tenderly.

"You know what I'd like before dinner?" She put a hand to his chest, loving that he was so physical. "A shower."

"Swim first?"

"I don't have a suit."

He grinned, lifting one eyebrow. "Private lake."

"Ah." She'd act as if skinny-dipping in daylight was something she did all the time. "Okay, then."

"I'll put some things in the refrigerator and join you."

"Let me help?"

"No. You go have fun." He shooed her out onto the side deck through the French doors in the large, airy kitchen.

Alana gave in and started for the lake, wondering how she'd survive those first weeks in Florida without this man she'd only known a few days. She'd been sure separation would quickly take care of the feelings they'd started. Now she wasn't sure at all. She enjoyed him so much—and being madly pampered wasn't bad, either.

She tramped down the path toward the narrow sandy beach where she'd have to get naked, peering around anxiously for stray hunters or nosy neighbors or armed psychotics.

Nothing but tiny waves rippling the lake's surface, a breeze that stiffened suddenly, keeping the worst of the mosquitoes away, and a small brown bird with a yellow beak hopping along the water's edge.

So. Apparently she was supposed to strip now.

Okay.

She pulled the yellow top over her head, folded and laid it neatly over a low tree branch, stepped out of her shorts, folded those and did the same. Glanced around nervously again, approached the water and tested it with her toe. Nice cool temperature; the air was warm enough this far inland that the lake would feel good on her stale sweat-dried skin, and the sun lowering in the sky was still strong enough to reheat her after she got out.

So.

Okay.

She unhooked her bra, keeping careful watch for trespassers, and turned to her clothes-hanger branch when something caught her eye up at the house.

Sawyer, staring through the French doors.

Pervert.

But knowing he was there keeping watch also made her feel safe. And daring. And yes, suddenly very ready to be naked.

She took off her bra, twirled it in circles over her head like a cowgirl stripper, and let it fly. Lifted her arms over her head and danced in a slow circle, undulating her hips, swinging her hair, then added a long topless shimmy facing the house, pretending she wasn't at all aware of him. For her next number, she covered her breasts with her hands and did a few boom-bada-boom moves, then slid fingers down and beyond, snagging her panties on the way.

Voila. Naked. She turned her back to the house, caressed her rear in luxurious circles while performing a slow, erotic buns-out version of the twist, taking her down almost to kneeling, then back up. Not even glancing behind her, she tossed her head and sauntered toward the water, hearing, too late, the thud of his feet coming after her.

She squealed and started to run, splashing through the shallows; he caught up with her, lifted her around the waist and dunked her with him.

"Argh!" Alana surfaced, dripping, giggling, energized by the cold. "Why you—"

She lunged and tackled him around the waist, scoring a direct hit and rewarded with his collapse into the water. She swam away, then around in a circle. He came up grinning, flung his head to the side to get hair off his face. "What were you trying to do with that striptease? Kill me?"

"Gee, Sawyer, I had no idea you were watching."

He splashed her in punishment. She giggled and dove under, feeling as if she were starring in one of those falling-in-love montages from a chick flick. Couple in a romantic French bistro, couple taking pictures along the beach, couple laughing and splashing naked in a lake. Later, couple in bed, making love.

Falling in love.

It could happen for her, too. It might have already. Right now, dripping wet and high on life, she cared less and less about stopping it anymore.

They swam for a while longer until hunger drove them back inside and into the shower. Scrubbed and shampooed and refreshed, she dragged on one of his T-shirts over clean panties and left her wardrobe change at that on his request, feeling sexy and comfortable and as if bliss was her new inseparable best friend.

They sat on the screened-in porch outdoors in cushioned Adirondack chairs, enjoying the breeze, protected from mosquitoes, drinking beer, eating the picnic Sawyer had packed: cold chicken flavored with soy sauce, ginger and garlic, Asian slaw, peanut noodles, watermelon and butterscotch brownies, then more beer, sitting with their feet up on the low table, sharing stories of their childhoods, enjoying the view of the setting sun turning the calm lake pink. Utter contentment.

"So...Alana."

"Mmm?"

"Just wanted to warn you, I'm planning to get you naked again very soon." He gestured toward her with his beer bottle. "Because looking at you in that T-shirt and panties has been pure pleasure, but it has also been pure torture."

"I see." His low, husky voice made her shift on her seat, nipples hardening under the soft cotton, which he immediately noticed and appreciated, which made her shift again.

"What do you think?"

"I think..." She sent him a smoldering come-hither look. "I need to powder my nose first."

He chuckled. "Second door on the right. The bedroom is the door on the left past it. I'll meet you."

"Deal." She kissed him and went into the bathroom, simply designed but top-quality like the rest of the house, from the enormous claw-foot tub to the stone vessel sink, to the toilet that barely made a sound when she flushed. A look in the mirror showed a very, very relaxed and happy woman. Today had been so perfect, from breakfast in bed to the museum, to lunch, to the, ahem, basement, then beach and now lake house.

Had she mentioned she could get used to this?

Three more days, give or take. Three more days to fall

harder for this amazing man, and then she'd get to rip out her heart and leave it with him when she left.

Florida. Most people thought of it as paradise. Right now it felt like jail.

She emerged from the bathroom into the dimly lit hallway and followed his directions toward the room with the glow of light spilling from under the nearly closed door which she lost no time in pushing open.

Candles. She stood and took in the scene. A dozen at least, at various locations behind and to the sides of the beautiful iron bed. On the polished wood mantel, on the bedside table, on the bookcase at the far wall, arranged on the low window seat. Her delighted laughter died the instant she looked at Sawyer.

He'd stripped to his boxers and stood by the bed, feet planted, hands loosely on his hips, chest and muscled arms lit to a golden glow. Shadows played on his cheekbones and strong jaw, his hair was carelessly tousled after his shower, but his gaze stopped her...from moving, from breathing. He watched her quietly, no grand gesture, but in his eyes she saw everything she'd ever wanted to see in a man's heart.

Come here. He didn't say it aloud, but held out his hand. She moved forward, feeling as if she were starring in one of her most perfect fantasies, except this was real. Even understanding that, part of her kept wanting to know for sure she wouldn't wake up and find out she'd been dreaming.

She stood opposite him. He put his hands to her waist and pulled her close, laid his cheek against her hair while she slid her fingers up the hard landscape of his arms. They stood like that she didn't know how long. His skin was warm on her temple, rough where his beard had emerged. Her breath was audible, catching occasionally, his deep and regular.

Then his lips touched her hair...her cheek...the corner of her mouth. Alana turned her face toward him and up; his lips brushed hers, drew back, brushed them again, making them tingle. She closed her eyes, trying to capture every sensation—his male scent, the hard heat of his muscles under her fingers, the warmth of his body so close, the soft tenderness of his lips, the acceleration in his breathing. His tongue drew a slow path across her mouth; he caught her lower lip between his, pulled gently, grazed it with his teeth. A shiver caught her, not from cold but from a necessary release of the building tension.

He pulled away; she opened her eyes and suddenly understood how it felt to drown in someone's gaze. Emotion swelled to the familiar point where she'd have to look away or be lost. A second before she gave in, he bent and kissed her, gently, then lingeringly, then harder, then with possessive passion that made her whimper and push close, feeling his erection bulging through the thin cotton of his boxers.

She loved the silence, loved the communication only through their bodies, loved the way she could immerse herself in sensing instead of speaking. He turned her toward the bed, arms locked around her, and supported her slow fall back onto the soft sheets, still kissing her, body wide and secure on top of hers. He lifted to help her out of the T-shirt; her breasts reacted to the cooler air in the room, which made his warm mouth warmer on them; her hands traveled the expanse of his back, solid under smooth masculine skin.

This man. This man. Everything about their time together was so much *more*. More romantic, more fun, more intense and so much more meaningful.

He slid her panties down her hips, helped their leisurely long journey off her legs by encouraging every few inches with gentle kisses, down her thighs, knees, calves, the soles of her feet. On the way back up, he stopped to explore with his tongue, slipping his finger inside her, bringing her to helpless gasps of pleasure while she alternately stroked and gripped his hair.

Then his boxers were gone. He rolled on a condom and lay back over her, supported on his elbows. His penis moved between her legs, anxious to gain entrance, but he took his time, patiently kissing her face and mouth again. She wound her hands around his arms, over his taut shoulders and not at all patiently pushed up her hips in silent invitation.

He accepted, slid inside her an inch at a time, pulling out in between advances so she really felt him stretching her, filling her. Then the final smooth slide to the hilt, and he started a slow and steady rhythm that made her clutch his biceps and grit her teeth to keep from crying out that he should go harder, get her to that peak she was so desperate for. She wanted their lovemaking at his pace, to satisfy his need, whatever he wanted. He'd given her the best day of her life. He'd given her candles and a bed with clean sheets. Everything else should be hers to give back to him.

He kept his pace leisurely, occasionally closing his eyes, pausing, then back to the easy gentle rhythm. Gradually she relaxed, arousal staying at a steady high simmer, stopped straining for her climax, loosened her grip on his arms and began a slow, sensual exploration of his body, stroking him everywhere she could reach.

In and out, in…and out, his buttock muscles contracting and releasing under her fingers. She resisted urging him on, opened her eyes and locked into his gaze. In spite of the intensity of their connection, physical and emotional, in spite of the feelings surging through her, or maybe because of them, she was finally content to watch him watching her, not a trace of panic, experiencing his slide inside her, the gentle friction he maintained by rolling and twisting his hips.

She had no idea how much time went by, maybe five minutes, maybe half an hour, maybe more. She could have stayed there forever, joined to this man so intimately, candles flickering, soft lake air caressing them through the open windows. Was this love? It didn't seem that it could be anything else.

Then he kissed her again, gentleness that soon gave way to the inevitable passion she both wanted and didn't. With desire's rise, his pace quickened, his thrusts became longer, harder, deeper. Ecstasy seemed to come at her from a great distance, like a storm's inevitable approach, closer and closer, more and more power evident, until that second of held-breath anticipation before the roaring rush of wind, thunder and rain.

She didn't think she'd ever come down, the orgasm went on and on, staying at its peak for an impossibly long time, during which she said his name in her mind over and over, aware of him inhaling sharply and coming to his own release.

When the intense pleasure finally let her go, she lay under him clasped in his arms, becoming dimly aware again of sounds and shapes and light around them.

"Alana." His voice was deep, quiet, full of longing.

She nodded. She understood. *I love you, too.*

She couldn't say it. Not yet. Too much at stake, too much still to work out. She hoped she'd shown him how she felt in every possible way while they were making love, so tenderly and so silently.

"That was…" He blew out a breath. "I hate the cliché, but I didn't know it could be like that."

"Me, neither." Afraid of love? No. She wasn't. The knowledge sat inside her, precious and shining, she hugged it tightly.

"So…Alana." Something about the way he said her name this time interrupted her dreamily relaxed mood.

"Yeah?"

He rolled off her, grabbed tissues and got rid of the condom with a perfect three-pointer into the trash can across the room, then lay back down and gathered her against his chest. "I've got a proposition."

The rest of her beautiful afterglow fantasy shattered. Oh, no. Not this argument again. She sighed and faked a return smile when he grinned at her. "Okay. Let's hear it."

"I was going to wait to tell you, but you should think this

over for the next few days while you're here. *If* I let you out of bed long enough."

She didn't need to fake the next smile. "O-kay…"

"If I take the job as director of the foundation, which it looks like I will, and if I can get the board of directors to go along with the low-rent studio idea, which I don't see why I wouldn't be able to, and if Debbie's partnership is amenable, which I'm sure they will be…" He lifted his eyebrows comically. "You with me?"

"Lots of *ifs*. I got that much."

"Lots of ifs." He pushed a hand through his hair, a lock of which ignored his efforts and tumbled back onto his forehead. "The new building…will need a manager."

It was suddenly hard to breathe.

"You're not only perfectly qualified for the job, but you'd be around working artists, and, I hope, get some of your soul fed in the process." His gaze turned sly. "At least better than managing condos in Florida."

"I've already committed myself." The protest was automatic. How many times had she made it?

"I know. Just think it over. Everything is in the planning stages so far, which accounts for all the ifs. For one, the building wouldn't be ready to manage for quite some time. It still needs buying and renovating. We're probably talking over a year. But if you stayed, I could find you work at the foundation. I spoke to my dad. He said the outgoing director is taking staff with him to his new job."

"I can't do this." She struggled onto her elbow. "Gran and Grandad—"

"Are healthier than you think."

"Even if that's true, they're not getting younger." The argument felt stale and false. Was she really thinking of them? Or was this knee-jerk self-protection?

"I thought they were in their late eighties the way you

talked about them, but your Gran sounded about sixty on the phone."

Alana swallowed. "She's seventy. Grandad is seventy-three."

"They could live another twenty years in perfect health." He narrowed his eyes but his voice was gentle. "If you don't want to do it, if there's some other reason, just say so."

"It's not that." She gestured meaninglessly and let her hand drop on his chest. "I just can't…I owe them so much. And you and I have known each other such a short time."

"I know. I'm asking a lot. A whole lot. All the risk would be on your side and that's not fair. I'm probably being selfish even bringing it up. I just want you to know the option is there, and that nothing would make me happier than if you agreed to stay." He kissed her, and she responded a little desperately, wishing they could go back to when they were making love and the rest of the world didn't exist. "I probably should have waited, but I'm so…excited I guess. Like a kid Christmas morning with a present he can't wait to give someone."

"That's very sweet." She hardly knew what she was saying. He'd been working hard behind the scenes to get her to stay. It felt wonderful…and also invasive. Was this how Melanie felt when Alana tried to guide—aka control—her life? She didn't like it, no matter how wonderful his intentions.

"But now maybe the present is the wrong size. Or you already have one. Or like the racing car I bought my mom when I was seven, maybe it's not something you want so much as I do."

She laughed through the growing anxiety. How could she make a decision like this? Pitting a man she loved but barely knew against grandparents she owed her life to. Ditching important plans she had in place on the whim of a too-new emotion? One thing to decide to stay on an extra day or two. But forever?

"Sawyer, I really don't see—"

"Shh." He covered her mouth with her favorite Mute button—his lips. "Don't think, don't worry, don't feel pressure to decide. Just let the idea settle for a while."

"But I— Mmph."

He kissed her again, rolled her under him, kissed her some more, long sensual kisses that blotted out any hope of continuing to reason.

But sooner or later she'd need to face up to this decision. She couldn't keep putting it off by spouting the same arguments for leaving while she'd continued to prolong her stay.

Either way she decided, she'd be choosing happiness, pain and also regret, possibly for the rest of her life.

14

"OH, COME ON, Alana, have a double." Melanie was already licking her two-scoop turtle sundae frozen custard cone: vanilla custard shot through with gooey thick threads of caramel and hot fudge, mixed with roasted salted pecan pieces. Her sister's insistence on denying herself pleasure made her insane. "Skip dessert at dinner, it all evens out."

"Oh, yeah?" Alana turned to the teenager behind the counter at Gilles frozen custard stand, a Wauwatosa institution since 1938, which claimed to be the area's oldest fast-food restaurant. "I'll have a double special flavor, too."

Melanie stopped mid-lick. "You will?"

Holy crapoly. They'd gone through the oh-have-a-double, no-no-I-couldn't charade for years. Alana had never given in. Sometimes she'd agree to share a sundae, but she always gave up a third of the way into it, boo-hoo, she might put on an entire ounce and a half. Melanie would shrug and inhale the rest herself, annoyed and betrayed. Woman's code of honor: if you decided to indulge in something bad for you with a friend, you had a solemn responsibility to hang in there to the bitter end.

Today Alana had barely hesitated before giving in. "Wow, what's gotten into my big sister?"

She shrugged, as if changing a lifetime habit overnight was no big deal. "I just felt like it."

"So…?"

"So what?" She accepted her cone, paid for hers and Melanie's.

"So what is different? You're eating more, looking absurdly happy, humming nonstop, gazing starry-eyed at nothing, gee, let me guess." She tapped a finger against her cheek. "Tonsilitis?"

"Hmph." Alana grabbed a few napkins, which Melanie always forgot to do, and they went outside to lean against Alana's car and enjoy the evening air with their million calories.

"So?"

"Melanie, if you have a question, ask me." She sounded severe, but couldn't stop smiling long enough to be convincing.

Melanie was delighted. Envious, but delighted. The Ice Princess had fallen. "You're finally in love."

"Finally?" She made an I-don't-think-so face. "Come on. I've been in love before."

"Nuh-uh." Melanie caught a drip on her tongue. "Not like this."

"It's the infatuation," Alana explained patiently, as if she was some kind of expert. "Love takes time to emerge from it. I've known Sawyer what, a week? Not even?"

"It doesn't take time when it's right."

Alana, predictably, made a face. "Look who's talking. You've fallen 'in love' a million times, usually in the first three minutes knowing a guy, and every time you're sure it's 'right.'"

Melanie shook her head. She'd done a lot of thinking in the past few days. A lot. "No, I've never been sure."

Alana deflated midrant. "What do you mean? You always say you are. You even had yourself half-engaged to Sawyer."

"I know, I know. But deep down? Really deep? I knew they weren't right. I've been thinking about this constantly, Alana, after Edgar brought it up. It makes so much sense. I go for deliberately inappropriate men to keep from having to be serious about any of them. You do it, too."

Alana started to make her protest noises, the kind she made when she needed to waste time faking outrage while thinking of a comeback. Then, incredibly, she stopped and sighed deeply. "Okay. Maybe."

Melanie nearly choked on her bite. Maybe? This was serious progress. "If you understand that about yourself, why are you still planning to move to Florida?"

"I agree that I've have dated men in the past who couldn't touch me. But Sawyer isn't one of them. I'm not moving out of fear. It's just…bad timing."

"It's *miraculous* timing. It's *meant-to-be* timing. You weren't even supposed to come up here. How many men like him do you think you'll meet in your life?"

"Oh, and you're an expert because…"

"Not because of *him*. Because of *you*, how you're acting. I've never seen you like this. You're smiling—"

"I smile a lot."

"—you're happy—"

"I've been happy plenty."

"—you're eating a *double cone*."

"Oh, *that's* concrete proof. How's this?" She held up her custard like a beacon, which Melanie loved because Alana was down over one scoop already, and was on course to finish her entire double without a single panic over calories. "I swear by the sacred double cone that I'm not afraid of love."

Melanie chuckled. Her sister was positively giddy. "Then stay and enjoy it."

"I can't." She lowered the cone, smile drooping. "I can't change my life based on a few wonderful days."

"A week. And why not?"

"All my plans. My future. Gran and Grandad—"

"Are not going to kick off in the next few months just because you're not there. You think they'd want you to turn your back on happiness for their sakes? You're doing it again, you know, ordering a single cone when you really want a double."

"Melanie…"

"The only reason you don't want to stay is because you know he's The One, so you're running away as fast as possible."

More outrage noises. Really good ones. "Why on *earth* would I do that to myself?"

"The same reason I slept with Sledge instead of pursuing someone who made more sense as a partner. But knowledge is power, and I'm changing my strategy." Melanie tapped her head smugly. "I made a list of everything I want in a guy. Then I crossed off the cosmetic ones. You know—heart-stoppingly gorgeous, loves to dance, penis the size of a salami."

"Shh." Alana peered around for anyone close enough to hear, giggling into her hand.

"And you know what I ended up with?" She stopped to let Alana enjoy the suspense, then her throat thickened and she couldn't make herself say his name. *Come on, Melanie.* "Edgar."

"What? You're mumbling."

"I said…Ed-gar."

Alana's eyes shot wide. "*Edgar?* That guy with the beyond-help hair?"

"Beyond-help." She shook her head sadly, feeling queasy.

"And zero fashion sense?"

"Negative fashion sense. That's the one."

"And a girlfriend." Alana crunched the first bite of her sugar cone. "Which makes him inappropriate, too."

"I know. Except for that part, though, he's it." Her voice was too high. She felt a little itchy.

Alana bit into her cone again. "He does have great eyes, Mel."

"Great eyes."

"And his body isn't bad at all."

"You noticed that?" She hunched and released her shoulders.

"I'm not dead. And—" Alana pushed hair back the wind had blown across her mouth "—if I didn't know he had a girlfriend, that one time I saw you together when we had lunch at Christmas, I would have said he's crazy about you."

"He's crazy about Emma." She laughed too loudly. She wasn't going to bother mentioning the distinct feeling she got at their last meeting that Alana could be right. Which made no sense, given how devoted he'd seemed to his girlfriend for so long. Maybe they were having problems?

"Have you ever met this Emma person?"

"Nope." Melanie licked her custard down flat to the cone, her appetite fading fast.

"Maybe he made her up."

"Ha! That's crazy." A hint of panic raised its pesky little head. "He talks about her all the time, stuff they did together, what movies they watched, what she thought of them, her favorite foods. And Sledge knows her. Said she has a lot of black hair."

"So do skunks."

Melanie had to cover her mouth to keep from spraying vanilla custard. She liked her sister again today, and that felt good.

"How did that guy get to be named Sledge anyway?"

"He wouldn't tell me. But…" Melanie leaned confidentially toward Alana, relieved at the subject change. "If you want my opinion, a girlfriend gave him the nickname."

"What makes you say that."

"Sledgehammer. In bed. He's a pounder."

"Ugh." Alana wrinkled her nose. "Men like that learned about sex watching porn."

"And they wonder why real women don't come, screaming, every five minutes." Melanie snorted. "'Because, honey, ya just smashed my pleasure button into numb pulp.'"

Alana nearly choked on her cone. She planted a hand on her chest and let go, laughing until her face turned red and tears ran down her face.

Melanie smiled, experiencing a rush of sisterly love. If Alana would be like this all the time, Melanie wanted her to stay in Milwaukee, too. They could actually have fun together, which they hadn't managed to since puberty hit. "I wish you wouldn't go, Alana."

Alana's laughter ran out of steam. "Aw, Mel."

"I'd like the chance to get closer. Six years ago when you left, I know it wasn't possible, but I feel as if now..."

"I know." Alana turned to hug her. "You and me?"

"You and me." Melanie squeezed her hard. She wanted so much for her sister to be happy with Sawyer. And she wouldn't mind being happy herself. At some point. With someone. They broke apart and leaned back against the car, resumed eating their cones, both crunching now, Melanie feeling relaxed again. Cars rushed by on Blue Mound. Customers came and went.

"What are you going to do about Edgar?"

"Oh. Well." She couldn't believe how she was reacting. On paper, her theories about Edgar as a romantic prospect had made so much sense. But sharing them with Alana was nerve-racking. "What are *you* going to do about Sawyer?"

"I'll think about staying." She put her hand up when Melanie snorted. "No, I really will, Mel. I even told Sawyer I would when he asked me to stay."

"He asked you to stay!" She socked her sister on the shoulder. "Why didn't you tell me? Oh my God, can I be bridesmaid at your wedding?"

"Ha." Instead of shrieking, Alana actually grinned. "Down, girl. He even lined up a job for me."

"Wow. *Wow.*" Melanie couldn't believe it. Sawyer was putting even more pressure on Alana than she was. She felt amateur in comparison. "So I guess you don't need me nagging you."

"Especially because it's my turn to nag. What about Edgar?"

"Oh. I don't know." She tried to pretend the last bit of her cone was fascinating while her stomach knotted up again. "I can't interfere with what he's got going with Emma."

"Who in two years you've never seen. Why don't you show up at his place after work? Say you were just in the neighborhood or visiting Sledge. Find out if Edgar has any skunks around." She started giggling again. "Or, God, what if Emma is *inflatable?*"

Melanie did spray custard that time, but not entirely from being amused. Alana laughed so hard a father and son nearby turned and smiled. Melanie hoped they wouldn't ask what was so funny.

"Well." Melanie forced another chuckle, wondering why she hadn't cracked up as hard as her sister. "There's a concept."

"I'm just saying…" Alana shook with a leftover giggle, then got herself back under control by licking the last of the custard off her fingers. "Seriously, go over there, tell him you decided you want to date someone more like him, and does he have any friends. His reaction will tell you everything you need to know."

"Yeah. Okay." Her stomach gave another unsettling tug. "On one condition."

Alana froze with her pinky still in her mouth. "Uh-oh."

"You stay another month."

"No."

"Two weeks."

"Melanie."

"A week and a half."

Alana pressed her lips together, but a smile threatened anyway. "Five days."

"A week, Alana. Come on. He's worth it."

"Maybe."

"Good." She finished her own cone and pushed away from the car, too twitchy to stand there anymore thinking about men. She wanted to go home, change and jog a few miles, get rid of this restless energy.

Tomorrow she'd visit Edgar after work. It did seem like a sensible idea, and she was trying very hard to be sensible. Plus, having decided to go, she might as well get it over with. She'd pretend to stay late at the office after he went home, or have a drink somewhere first, maybe with Jenny, to give Edgar time to settle in for the evening with Emma. Jenny could give her courage...or stop her by telling her she was crazy. That would work. And be so much easier.

Melanie climbed into Alana's passenger's seat, custard still turning traitor in her stomach. Her earlier conviction that this time she had it together and Alana was a mess had broken up and dissolved. She felt like her old messy self again. Hooray.

Alana started the car, pulled onto Blue Mound heading east toward Washington Heights and home. Melanie buckled up and leaned back in her seat, watching the neat rows of houses passing, tense with dread.

What happened if after all this progress it turned out that understanding her problems with men didn't bring her any closer to fixing them?

MELANIE WALKED DOWN Water Street, taking small precise steps. Six o'clock and she was exhausted. She'd been on time to work that morning, part of her new, more serious leaf-turning-over commitment, but there had been meetings and deadlines and a birthday lunch for Jenny's cubicle partner Doreen. Through it all she'd felt like she was high on something, but not pleasantly. Talking to Edgar had been torture, especially because of course he noticed the change and wanted to know what was wrong. She'd asked him about Emma, what had they done the previous evening? Watched TV on the couch, then he went to bed and read. Emma didn't read? No, she wasn't much of a reader. What did she do? Took a bath, then came to bed with him.

Emma sounded really boring.

But who was Melanie to judge? She'd gone after romantic thrills her whole life and never managed to be remotely happy.

Another block gone, another one to go; her steps got smaller. She hadn't found a miracle parking place this time. Was that a bad sign? She didn't know.

Another half block. His building grew as she got closer.

Maybe he wouldn't be home?

But then she'd have to come back sometime and that would suck.

She crossed East Erie Street, the last barrier, and made it up the steps to his front door. A few more steps and she was in the foyer, scanning the buzzers for his name. She pushed 3C with a shaky finger.

Waited.

"Oh, well." She turned away from the panel and made for the exit. Obviously he wasn't—

"Yeah?"

—home.

She sighed, turned back and approached the speaker. Time to live by her brave and noble words. "Hi, Edgar, it's Mel."

"Melanie." His voice softened into concern. "Are you okay?"

"Can I come in?"

"Um…yeah. Yeah, sure, come on up." The buzzer sounded, the door clicked unlocked. She pushed through and trudged up the stairs, wincing when she passed Sledge's door. Another flight and Edgar met her on the landing outside his apartment, took her arm anxiously.

"Did something happen? You've been acting strange all day."

Her stomach gave a little flutter, but she couldn't tell whether it was pleasure or dread. "I need to talk to you."

"Yes. Of course. Sure." He waited expectantly.

"Uh." She looked around the dingy stairwell. "Can we go into your apartment?"

"Yes." His voice was overly hearty. "Yes. Come on in."

Was his place a mess? Or was there another reason he didn't want her there? Had he not told Emma they were close friends? Were he and Emma about to have sex when she buzzed? *Was* Emma inflatable?

He pushed open his door and gestured her in. "After you."

His apartment was not what she expected. First, it was neat. Very neat. And clean. Scary clean. And elegant. Dark wood furniture; chairs and sofa with fabrics in shades of teal and burgundy and gold, even coordinating throw pillows; pots of plants and African sculptures on end tables and bookcases; Indian woven tapestries on the walls, which were a warm ochre color; a small fountain cascading water over pretty stones into a glazed bowl; a tank with colorful fish swimming happily around water plants. Brilliant use of the modest space so that even though the room was well-furnished, it didn't feel at all crowded.

Emma wasn't a skunk. She was a woman with incredibly sophisticated, international taste. Melanie had spent all these months—years, actually—thinking she was too cool for Edgar, and it might turn out to be the other way around.

She shouldn't have come.

"Edgar, your place is gorgeous. Look at this."

"Oh. Thanks. Thank you." He seemed nervous, rubbed

his hands on his bright green shorts, which he'd paired with a maroon T-shirt, shudder.

"Is Emma around?"

"No. No, she's not. Not sure where she is right now." He paced toward the kitchen, then came halfway back. "Do you want something to drink?"

"Oh, sure. Beer if you have it. If not—"

"I have it. Or wine. Or anything stronger."

"I'll take a beer, thanks, Edgar." She heard the sound of a refrigerator opening and even in her misery over discovering Edgar might be out of her league, she couldn't keep her curiosity at bay and followed.

His kitchen was gorgeous, too—professional range, impressive cookware hanging from an iron rack easy to reach from the stove. More plants by the window and on the solid, quality kitchen table. Why had she been so sure his place would look like a college dorm room?

"You and Emma must love to cook."

"I love to cook. Emma loves to eat." He poured salted almonds into a bowl, grabbed a bag of sweet potato chips from the cabinet and a dish of baby carrots from the refrigerator.

"Edgar, just the beer is fine."

"Oh." He stood holding the food, looking lost.

Melanie's heart lifted a little. He was still Edgar. "I'll take it in for you. It's nice of you to go to the trouble."

"For you it's no trouble."

"You're a sweetheart, Eddie." She sat on the spotless sofa, terrified she'd spill or leave crumbs, and hoisted her bottle, anxious to get those first calming sips down. Jenny hadn't wanted to go out after work, so Melanie had been rattling around her office cubicle for the past hour, working herself up into nervous misery. "Cheers."

He frowned. "Did you want a glass? Sorry, I didn't think—"

"No, this is fine." She put her hand on his arm, which always surprised her with its strength. "Really. Thank you."

"So? What's going on? You seemed distracted all day." He took a swig of beer and settled in as if she hadn't interrupted his evening unexpectedly, as if he had nothing to do for the rest of his life but listen to her.

Edgar was something really special.

"I'm fine, really. Today was stressful, that's all." She nodded stupidly, with no idea how to launch into what she wanted to say. He must have had an old-fashioned clock somewhere because she could suddenly hear it ticking.

"You...said you wanted to talk about something?"

"Yes. Yes." She held the bottle in her lap, not wanting to risk staining his coffee table. "I've been thinking a lot about what you said."

"About..."

"About me going for inappropriate men."

"And?"

"And I think you're right." She peeled off a piece of the beer's gold foil label. "I need to find someone different. For sure. I need to date someone...like...who is different."

She pushed the neck of the bottle back between her lips and gulped. Dammit, she couldn't do this. Everything was so weird with Edgar sitting right there close to her, not in a cubicle, not in a public restaurant, but on his turf, his and Emma's turf. He'd relaxed and she was still a complete wreck. She should have trusted her gut instinct that this was all wrong, instead of her intellect. Her id over her superego.

Except that same id was always the culprit when she got into trouble with no-good men.

This was horrible.

"I think that's great, Mel." He put his hand on her shoulder, rubbed gently. "I hate seeing you get hurt."

"Yeah, um, thanks." She blew her bangs out of her eyes. Worse and worse. She'd barged into his room and all she'd managed to say was, "I want to date different men"? He already knew that. And typical Edgar, even if he was thinking "Why the hell did you inflict yourself on my evening to tell me old news," he gave no sign of it.

She owed him the real story. *Edgar, you are so special and I think someone like you could make me really happy, and maybe I could make someone like you happy, too.*

"The thing is. Uh, I was thinking about what *kind* of man I'd want."

"Yeah? What kind?"

She forced herself to stop staring at the bottle in her lap, and looked up into his attentive, sweet, wonderful blue eyes. *Your kind.* "I was thinking I'd like to date someone like—"

The door burst open. "Hey man, sorry I took so long, they mixed up the order."

In walked a male body in black, carrying a pizza box. A pair of equally blue eyes, blazing with heat and curiosity and sex turned from Edgar to Melanie.

Melanie's jaw dropped. *Oh my God.* Her heart was already beating too fast from the awkward scene with Edgar, but it gave a valiant stab at speeding up even more. She tore her gaze down from those blue orbs of doom before she fell under their spell.

"Who's this?" The strong black-stubbled jaw tipped; black hair swung free over his ear. Was he checking her out? She didn't dare look higher to find out, so she looked lower. Black T-shirt tight over muscular chest. Black jeans tight over fabulous hips and legs. Black spiked belt, black motorcycle helmet clutched in black-gloved hand.

She kept her head down. She could not look at him again. She must not look at him. To look was to lust. After the mistake with Sledge, after all her subsequent soul-searching and self-discovery, she had to, *had* to have learned her lesson.

"Stoner." Edgar sounded as if he'd aged forty years. "This is Melanie."

"Yo, Melanie. Whassup?"

"Melanie." Edgar gestured to the sex-apparition and dropped his hand despondently on the sofa arm. "This is my brother, Stoner."

"Oh," she whispered. "Nice to meet you."

Nice was an understatement. He was cool water in a parched dessert, he was that first steak after Lent, he was a three-speed rotating vibrator in a girls-only dorm.

She was not going to look at him.

A meow sounded from beside the couch; a black cat stalked over and sniffed the newcomer's shiny black boots. Stoner crouched to pet her. "Hey there, sweet little Emma."

Melanie gasped and jerked to Edgar as if someone had slapped her. "You named your cat Emma?"

"Uh…" Edgar tried again to speak, then shook his head, looking as if someone had caught him across the windpipe.

From the corner of her eye, Melanie saw black gloves pick the cat up and stroke the length of its body.

Don't look. Don't look. Those hands…

"What's wrong with Edgar naming his cat Emma, Mel-a-nie?" His deep voice lilted seductively through the syllables of her name.

Melanie examined the hem of her shorts minutely. "Well. His. Um. Girlfriend is also named…"

Oh, no.

She turned back to Edgar. Emma had lots of black hair. Emma had simple needs. Emma wasn't much of a reader. Emma didn't cook but Emma liked to eat. Emma's taste was similar to Melanie's, which meant that necklace—

"His girlfriend?" Stoner swaggered toward Melanie, deposited the cat in her lap and made sure his thighs touched her knees, that his fingers brushed across her bare legs during the transfer. Tingles of electricity shimmied up her…everything. "Dude, Edgar, I didn't know you were seeing someone. All right."

He leaned over to high-five his brother. Melanie's heart broke. Edgar looked as if he wanted a wrecking ball to come through the wall so he could climb on and be swung away. "Oh, Edgar."

She stopped herself. She couldn't humiliate him in front of his unbelievably sexy brother.

"Sorry, I got confused." She laughed dorkily. "There's another guy at the office with a girlfriend named Emma. I mixed them up. Cat, girlfriend...I do that stuff all the time."

Edgar mouthed *thanks*. His eyes pleaded for forgiveness.

She'd forgive him. Though she might have to shriek at him in the best Hawthorne tradition first. Why on earth had he felt the need to pretend with *her*? Of all people. As if him being single would have made any diff—

Oh, no. If there was no Emma—as Alana suspected, and maybe Melanie did, too, deep down—that meant Edgar was totally available. That meant Melanie didn't have to date someone *like* Edgar.

She could date Edgar.

A powerful surge of panic drew her up off the couch. "I should go."

"Hey, pizza's here, beer's here." Stoner's hands landed on his hips. She was not going to examine what was between them. "And you're here, Mel-a-nie. I can't think of a better party."

"Oh. Thanks." Melanie headed for the door, eyes on the floor. "But I really—"

"Hey." Stoner stepped into her path with such graceful speed that she nearly bumped into him. "Don't go."

She mumbled an excuse, kept her head down. If she looked at him she was lost.

"Stay?" His voice was a sexy bad-boy's manipulative plea that made her want to wrap her legs around all that black and get shot to the moon.

She'd never be healthy, she'd never get it right, she'd never find the kind of love she dreamed about. Not as long as there were men in the world like Stoner who turned her upside down with a single glance.

"Okay. I'll stay." She gave in, looked up into his hot, melting, blue, blue eyes.

And fell deeply and forever in love.

Again.

15

Alana sprayed Windex on the outside of the storm window in her bedroom, balanced on the ledge, leaning out with the scrubber stuck on an extension pole, squeegee inside within easy reach. A fly buzzed past into her bedroom. The scrubber whooshed across months of dust and dirt cemented into place by raindrops and snowflakes. She changed tools and reached with the squeegee, missing spots, smudging others. Finally she jammed a paper towel on the end of the extension pole and tried to manipulate it into the corners, sweating and puffing in the heat and humidity.

Yup. Windows. She'd gone over the edge.

If this was love, she'd rather go back to shallow infatuation. Melanie might have figured out everything about herself and about Alana, but it hadn't helped her any, either. Emma was apparently a cat, which meant Edgar, her best friend, had been lying to her for two years; Edgar's brother was so sexy Melanie had wanted to drop her pants right there in Edgar's apartment; and after all her theorizing, she hadn't been able to bring herself to tell Edgar what was on her mind even when she had the chance. To say she was discouraged was an understatement. She'd even been on time for work again today because she hadn't been able to sleep.

So, for sake of argument—which argument Alana had been having in her head for the past two days, which was what made window-washing start to look pretty good—what if Melanie was right, and Alana was operating out of fear of commitment? What if she were moving to Florida because she was scared of her feelings for Sawyer, scared of the vulnerability, scared of the potential for pain, of losing herself inside a man the way Melanie constantly did, the way their mother had, over and over?

What then? She couldn't fix it by wanting to. And she wasn't willing to stay in town for years of therapy while she tried.

On the other side of that same coin, what if she really was leaving because subconsciously she knew staying even for someone as wonderful as Sawyer wasn't what she truly wanted? Maybe she knew she'd worry about her grandparents 24/7 and hate herself for sacrificing them to her desire for hot sex.

No, of course, Sawyer wasn't just about hot sex, though, um, yes, mmm. Even plain vanilla sex had been beyond anything she'd ever experienced.

Because he was a skilled lover? Because she was wildly in lust? Because this was really forever-love?

Where the hell was the manual that came with emotions? Page four: if you experience this-and-such and that-and-so-on then definitely yes, do this-'n-that. Oh, that would be so nice.

In the meantime, she had raging confusion, nightly sleeping pills—except that one night at the lake house in Sawyer's arms when she'd slept like a baby—and...windows.

The phone rang; she bumped her head coming back inside, then scraped her hip climbing back onto the floor, and nearly tripped racing for Betty Boop. "Hello?"

"'Lana, 's Mel."

"Melanie?" She put her finger in her free ear and bent

forward in that stupid way people did, as if being closer to the ground would help them hear better. Was her sister drunk? "You okay?"

"M'm's her'." She sounded as if she were talking through her teeth.

"What? I can't understand you."

"I s'd *M'm's her'*."

"What?"

"Hang on." Rustling sounds. Murmured words. Walking sounds. What the—

"Alana?" Her voice was clear now, but echoing.

"Melanie, what is going on?"

"I couldn't talk before—she was with Edgar—I said the boss was calling so I could—she just showed up—I can't believe—she looks totally—"

"Wait, whoa, calm down. I can barely understand you. Start over. Who showed up, a real Emma?"

"No, not Emma. *Mom*."

Air entered Alana's mouth in a weak gasp. She sank onto Melanie's bed and jumped up again when something sharp poked her. *"Mom? Our* mom? Is *there?* With *you? Now?"*

"She just showed up at work out of the blue, *bang,* like that."

"Oh my God." She turned, groped on Melanie's bed, flung a hanger off onto the floor and sank down again…then jumped up and started pacing. "Why didn't she come here to the house?"

"She doesn't know—she didn't know you were there. I told her. She's going to come see you next."

"Oh my God." She closed her eyes. More emotional confusion. On the one hand, Tricia was her mother. There had been happy times together, and in her own odd way, Alana was sure she loved her daughters.

But. There was another hand, and on it was years of neglect that bordered on abuse.

Forget windows. Alana was going to flip out the rest of the way and start scrubbing baseboard corners with an old toothbrush.

"She says she's turned over a new leaf, Alana."

"*That* sounds familiar."

"Ha, ha. She wants to spend time with us. To get to know us again."

"That does *not* sound familiar. How much time?"

"I...wasn't real clear on that."

"Oh my God."

"She does *look* different, anyway. She's wearing a normal nice sundress, no cleavage, no bared legs, but it's not a flower-child hippie caftan, either. It looks like it could have come from Talbots."

"Oh my *God*." She paced harder, tapping her fist against her lower lip. "Where is she planning on staying?"

"You don't want to know."

"Oh my—"

"Alana? You'd make me feel a whole lot better if you'd say something helpful instead of 'Oh my God.'"

"Yes. Sorry. I'm just..." she whirled around, clasping her head with her free hand "...trying to take this in."

"I know! I was sitting at my cubicle. I looked up and there she was. I nearly had a heart attack. Hang on. *Be out in a second.*"

"Out?"

"I'm in the bathroom. I wanted to warn you where she couldn't hear me."

"Thank you. I guess."

"Oh, I think she's talked to Gran and Grandad recently, too. Something she said made me think she had."

"What did—"

"I really have to go. Talk to you later."

"Mel, thanks for the—" the phone clicked off "—warning."

One more time: *Oh my God.*

She hung Betty Boop's receiver next to her beautiful plastic cartoon self, and wandered in a daze back to her half-cleaned windows. Three minutes later, she'd gone no farther than staring at the one she'd been in the middle of squeegeeing when Melanie called.

What was she going to do? About anything? Melanie, Gran and Grandad, Sawyer and now Mom. Alana felt responsible for all of their happiness and she didn't know what to do to guarantee any of it. She was terrified Melanie was going to go for this Stoner person over poor lovesick Edgar. She was terrified Gran and Grandad would go downhill if she weren't there to take care of them, no matter how often Mel and Sawyer said they didn't need her. She was terrified Sawyer's heart would break if she left town. And what did Mom want? Reconciliation? Disappearing years ago and now waltzing back in and expecting to take up where she left off? Was Alana supposed to bury all her resentment to make Mom happy, too?

Alana groaned and dropped her head into her hands. Back to where she started from. What did *Alana* want?

She wanted to talk to Sawyer.

He picked up after the first ring. Hearing his voice made her shaky with relief and teary and happy at the same time.

Love was just plain screwed up.

"Hey, there." He sounded so glad to hear from her that her shakiness began to steady into warmth. "What's going on?"

"Where do I start?"

"Uh-oh, that bad? Hang on, I'm in my car, let me pull over."

"You on your way home? It can wait."

"No, I'm on my way downtown to meet with the foundation board of directors."

"Doh." She whacked herself in the forehead. "I'm sorry, I knew that. You don't need me bothering you. Seriously, I'm fine, I don't—"

"You don't think you're more important to me than some board of directors?"

"Oh." She closed her eyes, surprised she could continue to stand upright since she'd just turned into goo. "Well…okay. My mom is in town. She's decided to reinsert herself into our lives."

"Whoa." He whistled. "That's intense. I take it you're not in the mood to let her in?"

"I'm…no. I guess I'm really not." Her voice trembled; she felt a retroactive burst of anger. "But even though she rejected us, I feel like I can't reject her. She's my mom."

"So on top of Melanie going nuts over another idiot, and me making your life miserable—"

"Ha." She fell back onto her bed, managing a smile even though not a single one of her problems had been solved. "You don't make me miserable."

"Well, that's progress."

She giggled. She'd never thought of herself as a giggler, but Sawyer had turned her into one. Could she really stand moving to that hot buggy state and that small soulless condo and living life for her grandparents?

Could she really stand to stay here and ignore their eventual decline?

"All you owe her, Alana, is to listen. You're an adult. It's up to you whether you want her back in your life or not. I'd be willing to bet she knows that, and knows she's been a pretty piss-poor mother. It's brave of her to show up and try to make it right. Maybe if you thought about it that way…"

She breathed in until her shoulders nearly touched her ears. He was right. He was very right. And very wise. And she was crazy about him. "Yes. I'll try that. It might help, thank you."

"And if she turns out to be looking for money or some other handout you don't want to give her, let me know and I'll send some boys to work her over."

Alana burst out laughing. "Nothing like a good pounding to help people see your point of view?"

"That's what I've always said. Though it hasn't worked on you yet."

"Ha. You're hardly a pounder." She rolled over onto her stomach, stroked the pillow as if he were there with her.

"Not even a quarter pounder?"

She laughed helplessly. Even his stupid jokes were funny to her. She had it bad. "Thank you, Sawyer. I really do feel better."

"I'm glad." He *was* glad, she could hear it in his voice—his pain for her, his caring, his empathy. Did she mention she was crazy about him?

"Good luck with your complete rubber stamp of a job interview today."

"I don't even think there's another candidate. My dad…" He snorted. "Well, I'm going to do a really good job. I'm not sure it's the job he thinks I'm going to do, but…"

"Can you get the foundation board on your side for the change of course?"

"I have a pretty good chance. I did research and most of them support the arts community in Milwaukee in some way or the other, either privately or through their companies. I'll go slowly at first. Get them behind this one project while continuing on our same path for now."

"Then hit them when they least expect it?"

"You got it."

She smiled dreamily. "Very schmaht."

"And of course I'll mention that I have a brilliant woman in mind who is trying to disentangle herself from pesky prior commitments to help me in a temporary capacity…"

Alana closed her eyes while her smile died a thousand deaths. So easy. It would be so easy to say yes, go ahead. But she wasn't yet sure.

"Why don't you call your grandparents, Alana. Level with

them. Tell them about me, tell them about the job, tell them about your concerns for them. See what they say."

She gave the pillow a whack of frustration. "I *know* what they'll say. They'll tell me to stay here even if they need me, even if my not coming would disappoint them terribly."

"You might be...surprised."

She shook her head. That wasn't the way to go. If only there were someone else who could talk to them, someone they could be completely honest with. Like...

Like...

The doorbell rang. She kept her voice calm, wished Sawyer luck with the interview, then got off the phone and glanced in the mirror, smoothed her hair, tucked in her shirt, then made a face and pulled it out again, re-messed her hair, went downstairs.

Like...her mother.

At the front door, even though the doorbell rang again, she hesitated. Bless Melanie for warning her, but it might have been kinder to let Alana suffer through the shock than this agony of dread.

One...two...three. She reached for the doorknob at the same time she caught sight of the picture on the foyer wall. Melanie, Gran, Grandad...and Mom. Smiling. Embracing.

Her family.

On that same beach, she now had pictures of Sawyer and herself. If only all six of them plus whatever disaster Melanie hooked up with could manage to live life peacefully and constructively close to each other. As a family.

She braced herself and opened the door to the mother she hadn't seen in four years. Her first impression was that Mom looked the same. Older, but then so was Alana. Her second impression was, as Melanie had said, that her mother looked totally different. Older not only in years, but in peace and maturity, too. Tasteful makeup, and her hair was no longer a dragging mop, but cut short and attractively in a style that flattered her small features. Her dress was green and pale yellow with small patches of light blue, and it suited her reddish-blond hair and greenish eyes. It suited her person, too—youthful without being ridiculously young, like the stomach-baring jeans she'd worn on the last trip when she was pushing fifty.

Melanie's eyes, Melanie's hair, Melanie's mouth, Alana's feminine body.

"Hi."

"Sweetheart. Alana." Her mother's eyes filled with tears, but she obviously knew better than to offer a hug. "Melanie told you I was coming. Warned you, I suppose."

"Yes." She stood a second longer, then couldn't stand being so rude and stepped back, gesturing her mother into the house.

Of course the first thing her mother noticed was the picture. She peered at it closely for a while—still too vain for glasses—and tapped on the frame. "Happy times."

"Mmm." She wasn't going to commit one way or the other. That had been a happy time, yes, but mostly because there was so much empty-of-Mom time surrounding it.

"The house looks good. Clean. You must have done that." She turned suddenly. Alana had forgotten the way she darted and swooped, like a hummingbird. Or a wasp. "Who's in my old room?"

"Guest room still."

"Ah, yeah. Okay." She flew into the living room, stood in the center, seemingly lost in thought. Alana found herself wanting to know what kind of growing-up memories she was reliving, but didn't want to ask. "I talked to Mom and Dad last night, Alana. We had a long talk. I told them I was coming home to Milwaukee for a while. They said you're moving down there in a few days?"

"Yes." Her voice came out husky and she had to clear her throat. "Yes, I am."

"Melanie says you have a new boyfriend here, though. A serious one."

"Yup." She folded her arms across her chest as if daring her mother to bring up any obvious issues or questions. Alana had enough people to discuss her troubles with.

"Getting straight to the point." She took a quick step toward Alana. "I know I wasn't a good mother. But I'd like to make it up to you now."

"Thanks, but…I don't really need a mother anymore."

"Everyone needs a mother."

"I'm leaving in a few days."

"Alana…" She reached out a hand, took a deep breath. "I'm starting over. I need your help, yours and Melanie's. I need you not to judge me for who I was, but who I'm trying to become. Melanie said she's trying to start over, too. She and I…I guess we're similar. Some things you don't want to pass along to your kids. I don't worry about her, though. No matter what crap she piles all over herself, she'll always find a way to crawl out. But you…"

"Me?" Mom wasn't as worried about sister screwup as she was about her sensible, capable older daughter? It just figured.

"I left you in charge. I made you grow up way too soon. You deserve some childhood now, a time to indulge yourself. You don't need to spend the rest of your youth taking care of your gran and grandad, Alana."

"So everyone keeps saying."

"Not because they don't need you, though I don't think they do quite yet." She pressed her lips together as if she were amused, but Alana wasn't in the mood to ask what was so funny.

"Then why?"

Tricia stood straight and tall with her arms at her sides, weight evenly distributed, and it occurred to Alana she'd always seen her mom leaning or curving or holding on to someone or something. She looked alone this way…but also stronger. "After I spend time here getting to know my daughters again, I am moving down to Orlando. Because taking care of my parents is my job, and I think it's about time I did my job. Your grandparents agree. Don't you?"

Alana stared, blinked, stared again. There was no way her mother could manage taking care of herself, let alone taking care of Gran and Grandad. The idea was ridiculous. No one could change that much.

I need you not to judge me for who I was, but who I'm trying to become. Your grandparents agree…

If Mom went down to take care of Gran and Grandad, Alana would be able to stay here in the city she loved. Working with artists at a job she already knew she enjoyed. She'd be here for Melanie, too, who needed her even if she'd rather eat rats than admit it. And…there would be nothing standing in the way of a commitment to Sawyer.

Commitment. To one man. Maybe for the rest of her life.

She put a hand to her chest as a rush of emotion nearly lifted her off her feet.

SAWYER PULLED his car opposite the house on Betsy Ross Place. His interview had gone surprisingly well. Surprising since half his mind had been on Alana the entire time. He was worried about her, both for her own sake and for his. Her mother planning to stay in the area could easily tip the balance toward Alana leaving for Florida. What if palmetto bugs were more appealing than reconciling with Tricia Hawthorne?

He wanted to meet this woman. Not hoping to become her son-in-law—he'd only been about ninety percent kidding about wanting to work her over for what she'd done to her daughters—but to get a better sense of her and whether the relationship with her daughters was salvageable. Being human was the sad fate of most humans, but the ones who really wanted to could change. Alana was changing, he felt that about her—she was loosening, relaxing. Maybe even Melanie could change someday.

Or maybe not. But it was possible Mom Hawthorne could redeem herself. He hoped so. By making peace with her daughters, she'd fill a gaping hole in Alana's life. He knew how much better he felt finding a job solution that would please both himself and his father. Jeremy Kern had for once called Sawyer instead of his brothers to talk about the prospects for the foundation, and then actually backed down on a few points when Sawyer held his ground.

With reformed mother and dutiful daughter reconciled, Alana might even be able to eject her baggage about letting him all the way into her life. There was definitely hope.

He reached into the backseat and pulled out the basket of flowers he'd bought impulsively from a florist on his way out of town. The riotous bouquet of blues and greens reminded him of Alana in the dress he'd bought her—and yeah, of the way she looked when she pulled off that dress and flung it across his basement.

Plus he was getting desperate. Maybe she needed several pounds of chocolate? A diamond bracelet?

She wasn't the type to be swayed by gifts, which was one of the things he loved about her. But getting her to stay would sure as hell be easier if she were bribable.

Grinning in the now-familiar driveway, he got out of the car next to Alana's Prius and tried to peer through the garage windows to see who else was home. Who knew what her mother drove, or whether she'd taken a cab. Melanie was probably still at work.

He really wanted the chance to talk to Alana alone. Life had been busy since that blissful day at the lake. They'd been all over together photographing and enjoying the city, and when they weren't doing *that,* he'd been involved in his woodworking class and Habitat one afternoon and a lot of meetings and phone calls, and when he wasn't doing that, he'd been researching how much sex two people could cram into each twenty-four-hour period.

A lot. All of it good. All of it pulling him deeper and deeper into certainty that Alana was the woman he wanted to spend the rest of his life with.

If he could just get her to stay.

He used his key in the back door, pushed it open, listening before he called out, in case Alana and her mother were talking privately and didn't need to be interrupted.

Nothing. He put the flowers on the kitchen table. "Alana?"

No answer. Was she in the shower? He took off his suit jacket, loosened his tie, poured himself a glass of water and gulped thirstily. Suits should be outlawed in the summertime.

"Anyone home?"

Still no answer. He was disappointed and slightly disconcerted. Maybe she was taking a walk? Though in this heat, he didn't see the point. Was she on the phone upstairs? The telephone here wasn't blinking In Use but maybe she was on her cell.

He walked through the kitchen door, down the hallway, up the stairs, peeked into the bedroom that used to be hers but was currently his—the room they'd shared their first night together, heavily drugged.

The shades were drawn, the room dim and quiet. But on the bed, a long Alana-shaped lump under the sheet. Exactly how she must have looked the first night he stumbled in here and didn't notice her.

He was about to back out, tenderly leaving her to the sleep she obviously needed after her encounter with her mother, when she moved—a leg, then an arm—and made that small sleepy sound that had woken him that first night when the drug had started wearing off.

There was no way he could walk out now. He was drawn

to her like an addict to his fix. At the side of the bed, he sat and watched. The curve of her bare shoulder, the cascade of her hair, the gentle rise and fall of her midsection.

This was one beautiful, sweet and supremely hot woman. If she left him, he'd shrivel like a grape left on the vine, surrendering his full, ripe prime to dried-up raisinhood.

She moved again, made another soft noise, and Sawyer was undone. He leaned forward to plant a soft kiss on the smooth skin of her upper arm, when suddenly the sheet was swept back.

He made a choked sound of surprise.

His sweet soft angel was wearing a black lace bustier, black lace garter belt, black fishnet stockings and, incredibly, black stiletto ankle boots.

"Hey there." She smiled with the innocence of a woman who's been around the block enough times to make it dizzy. "I've been expecting you."

He gaped like a fool. A fool whose pants were getting more and more uncomfortable by the second.

"Alana. You were— I mean, you weren't— Mmph." She threw her arms around him, caught him in a kiss and pulled him back onto the mattress.

"No, I wasn't." Long legs, tanned, muscled, capped with the outrageously sexy shoes lifted, extended and landed, bent and apart, on the bed. "How was your day?"

"Uh…" His voice cracked like an adolescent's. "Getting better all the time."

"Mmm, I'm glad. Tell me more."

"Um…it was…oh, man…wait a second." He made it off the bed away from her, but only to take off his clothes, unable to takes his eyes off her. That first night he'd compared her to a black-and-white movie star. Now she was a black-and-white version of the best sexual fantasy he'd ever had.

She rolled to her side, her breasts pushed tantalizingly together in the dark lace cups of the bra, and blinked sweetly. "Think you'll get the job?"

"Uh. Don't know yet." His shoes were gone. Socks: gone. Pants: gone. Brain: half-gone. Bed and candles had been fabulous, he had no problem whatsoever with bed and candles, but whatever had gotten into her today worked fine for him, too. Just fine.

"Well." She stroked her fingers up and down the valley of her cleavage. "Be sure to let me know of any new developments."

He made an incoherent sound and threw himself back onto the bed, stroking every inch of her smooth curves. "I think there's going to be a new development in about thirty seconds."

She grinned wickedly, produced a condom from somewhere, who knew, at this point he could barely see, then pushed him on his back and straddled him, lowered herself slowly.

There would never be another woman for him. He knew it as surely as he knew he was going to last an embarrassingly short time, because her hotter-than-hot outfit and lack of inhibition was making any attempt at control beyond him. She started to move, up and down, swinging her hair, arching her back. *Oh, man. Oh, no.*

He tried to say his five-times table and couldn't remember a single one. Five times Alana equaled…Alana. Five time sex equaled…more sex. He needed to slow down, make this good for her.

She closed her eyes, raised her arms, crossed them behind her head, riding him with new possessive confidence that was as much of a turn-on as the way she looked.

Gone. He groaned and came in bursts that made his whole body shudder.

Oh, no. Not since he was a teenager… "Alana. I'm sorry. You were so incredible, I couldn't hold back."

She grinned languorously, collapsed onto his chest, breathing hard, eyes closed, hair tumbling, cheeks pink. "Yeah, gee, Sawyer, I'm really annoyed that you found me so sexy."

"Damn, woman." He wiped his hand over his forehead, filmed with sweat. "Where did you get those shoes?"

"They're Melanie's."

"Ah." He grinned, still slightly out of breath. "So you *are* more like her than everyone thought."

She looked at him oddly. "What do you mean?"

"Your gran said you two were more similar than you knew."

"Hmm…maybe." She kissed him, kissed him again, dragged her tongue across his lower lip. "Except for one ver-r-ry important difference."

His body felt as if it had weights on it; he'd been pretty sure his drive was spent by that atomic blast of an orgasm, but the more she kissed him, the more he became conscious again of those miraculous black-lace-clad breasts against his chest and those hot-as-hell shoes, and the more he thought round two wasn't out of the question after all. "What difference?"

"*Melanie* is afraid of commitment. It's why her relationships are all disasters."

He pulled back, trying to pay close attention, at the same time he couldn't help running his hands up and down her gorgeous firm—

He suddenly heard what she hadn't said.

"You're not afraid of commitment?"

"Nope." She nuzzled his neck, bit gently, then soothed the spot with her lips and tongue. His libido definitely noticed that. "To prove it, I plan to commit myself immediately."

"Alana." He was split in three—his head was paying attention to her words, his heart was paying attention to their meaning, his other head was paying attention only to her beautiful body. "What are you saying?"

"I love you." She grinned at what must be the same stunned

look she was wearing at Bradford beach when he used the same words. "And I'm not going to Florida."

"You're—" He could barely believe that what he'd wanted for what seemed like years but was only a little over a week— God, could that be right?—was about to come true. "You changed your mind?"

"I'm staying here."

"Alana." He crushed her to him, had to loosen his grip when she made suffocation noises against his shoulder. "What finally persuaded you?"

"Mom. She's planning to stay awhile for the whole reconciliation project, then *she's* going to Florida to take care of Gran and Grandad. When she told me, I felt the most amazing relief. And I realized that I wasn't afraid of what was between us, I was afraid of not holding up my end of family responsibility."

"Alana, you've been doing that your whole life." He shook his head. Too many sacrifices, too hard and serious a life. If she'd let him, he'd spoil her rotten. Maybe even if she didn't let him.

"I know. But I'm ready to stop." She made a face. "Okay, well, I might have to help steer Melanie away from Stoner first."

"Agreed." He smoothed her beautiful dark hair back off her forehead. "But you'll have me to help."

Her smile made his whole world bright with possibilities it hadn't had for a long time.

"So if you're not going to Florida, how about somewhere else?" He lowered his hands to her hips and started her rocking back and forth again, heart full of what he wanted to say, though he knew she wasn't ready to hear it yet. But he also felt with every instinct he possessed that it was only a matter of time before she was. "I'm thinking St. Thomas."

"Us?"

"Mmm."

"Ooh."

"What would you think of it being our honeymoon?"

She started; her eyes went wide with shock.

He burst out laughing, unable to help it. Dirty trick. "I'm sorry, *how* not afraid of commitment are you?"

"I…we…it's…"

He rolled her over, kissed her sweet, perfect mouth. "You know, now that you've given in to staying in Milwaukee, I'm thinking I need something new I can convince you to do."

"Oh?" She locked her arms around him as he nestled between her legs where he belonged.

"What do you think? You stay in town and I'll work on you, slow and steady, until you agree to marry me."

She laughed, her eyes lit, cheeks turned pink with happiness—the sight he wanted to see every day for the rest of his life. "Sawyer, I can't commit to *anything*…better than that."

* * * * *

We hope you enjoyed Alana's story!
Find out what happens to her sister,
Melanie, next month in
Surprise Me… *by Isabel Sharpe.*
On sale from Blaze® in March 2011.

THE DRIFTER & TAKE ME IF YOU DARE
(2-IN-1 ANTHOLOGY)
BY KATE HOFFMANN & CANDACE HAVENS

The Drifter

Charlie Templeton is a wanderer, an adventurer. But one thing scares him: the chance that he's permanently lost the woman he loved, the woman he left. He's going back to Eve...

Take Me If You Dare

Mariska Stonegate's new man is secretly a CIA agent on the run. And he'll do just about anything to stay alive, including seducing Mariska one hot, steamy night at a time!

AMBUSHED!
BY VICKI LEWIS THOMPSON

Gabe Chance is blown away by the feisty redhead who unexpectedly lands right in his bed and, soon enough, his heart! He realises that Morgan's everything he wants, but she may be attracted by his ranch...

SURPRISE ME...
BY ISABEL SHARPE

Seduced by his fantasy woman. She's overlooked his intellect and dodgy haircut. He's totally in love; until he realises *she thought she'd climbed into bed with his bad-boy brother*!

are proud to present our...

Book of the Month

Walk on the Wild Side
by Natalie Anderson

from Mills & Boon® RIVA™

Jack Greene has Kelsi throwing caution to the wind
—it's hard to stay grounded with a man who turns
your world upside down! Until they crash with
a bump—of the baby kind...

Available 4th February

Something to say about our Book of the Month?
Tell us what you think!

millsandboon.co.uk/community
facebook.com/romancehq
twitter.com/millsandboonuk

One night with a hot-blooded male!

18th February 2011

18th March 2011

15th April 2011

20th May 2011

www.millsandboon.co.uk

THE *Royal*
HOUSE OF NIROLI

*The richest royal family in the world—united by blood
and passion, torn apart by deceit and desire*

The Royal House of Niroli: Scandalous Seductions
Penny Jordan & Melanie Milburne
Available 17th December 2010

The Royal House of Niroli: Billion Dollar Bargains
Carol Marinelli & Natasha Oakley
Available 21st January 2011

The Royal House of Niroli: Innocent Mistresses
Susan Stephens & Robyn Donald
Available 18th February 2011

The Royal House of Niroli: Secret Heirs
Raye Morgan & Penny Jordan
Available 18th March 2011

Collect all four!

2 FREE BOOKS
AND A SURPRISE GIFT

We would like to take this opportunity to thank you for reading this Mills & Boon® book by offering you the chance to take TWO more specially selected titles from the Blaze® series absolutely FREE! We're also making this offer to introduce you to the benefits of the Mills & Boon® Book Club™—

- **FREE home delivery**
- **FREE gifts and competitions**
- **FREE monthly Newsletter**
- **Exclusive Mills & Boon Book Club offers**
- **Books available before they're in the shops**

Accepting these FREE books and gift places you under no obligation to buy, you may cancel at any time, even after receiving your free books. Simply complete your details below and return the entire page to the address below. You don't even need a stamp!

YES Please send me 2 free Blaze books and a surprise gift. I understand that unless you hear from me, I will receive 3 superb new books every month, including a 2-in-1 book priced at £5.30 and two single books priced at £3.30 each, postage and packing free. I am under no obligation to purchase any books and may cancel my subscription at any time. The free books and gift will be mine to keep in any case.

Ms/Mrs/Miss/Mr_____ Initials _____

_____

Surname _____

Address _____

_____

_____ Postcode _____

E-mail _____

Send this whole page to: Mills & Boon Book Club, Free Book Offer, FREEPOST NAT 10298, Richmond, TW9 1BR